Copyright © 2025 by Rachel Marissa

All rights reserved

No part of this publication may be reproduced, distributed, or transmitted in any form or by any means, including photocopying, recording, or other electronic or mechanical methods, without the publisher's prior written permission, except as permitted by U.S. copyright law.

The story, all names, characters, and incidents portrayed in this production are fictitious. No identification with actual persons (living or deceased), places, buildings, or products is intended or should be inferred.

THE HEALING MANIFESTO

A Healing Romance

This time, grace.

For the younger me.

1 | ELISEO

The winter wasn't just cold. It was something else, something sharp, something brutal. The kind that made bones ache and air taste like metal. It gnawed at the skin, curled around the edges of breath, and crept in where coats and scarves were supposed to guard. It was the kind of cold that made a man wonder if his body was truly his own or if the frost had taken possession of it.

Eliseo hated it.

It was one of the big reasons he rarely came back to his hometown. The winter extended far past its supposed end date, a constant reminder that this place could strip you bare for far longer than one ever thought.

And yet, there she was.

No coat, no gloves, no hat. Just a t-shirt and sweatpants, rocking back and forth on the stone lip of the Slade Tarver Bridge, her hands gripping the edge like she wasn't sure whether to let go or hold on. She should've been shaking and wrapping her arms around herself, but she wasn't. The wind howled past, furious at her rebellion.

He slowed the car without thinking, watching her through the passenger window, expecting and hoping someone else would notice, that another car would honk, and that the world would react. But it was just him and the cold and this girl on the edge of something terrible.

Then she moved. Forward. Then back. Too fluid. Too practiced. The way someone tests a thing before trusting it. Before falling into it.

Something in Eliseo stilled. His mind tried to dismiss it, to push the thought away as too dramatic, too unlikely, but his body knew. Some marrow-deep knowing settled into him before the thought had words. He turned the car around.

By the time he pulled over, she was leaning again. Too close.

He stepped out, breath curling thick in the air, feet moving before he knew what to say. "Hey," he called out, voice low and careful. "You're not… you're not thinking about jumping, are you?"

Silence.

He swallowed hard. "Because there's always a better way. No matter what the problem is, it's not worth your life."

Still, nothing. She stared out at the dark stretch of water below, fingers tightening, muscles coiling like she was bracing herself for flight. He was afraid to move too fast, afraid to speak too loud, afraid that the wrong word might break whatever fragile thread was keeping her there.

And then she turned.

His breath caught. "… Juliana?"

She blinked. The name landed between them like a fallen stone, rippling outward and disturbing the stillness. Recognition widened her gaze, and suddenly, the cold didn't exist. The bridge didn't exist. Only the past. The laughter. The smell of flowers lingering in her room. Her legs draped over his as he read to her.

Then she looked away, and the world crashed back in. The bridge. The cold. The way her body was angled toward the fall.

"What are you doing?" Eliseo's voice was smaller now.

She exhaled, long and tired.

A kind of grief took hold of him, sudden and violent. This was Juliana Ward. The girl who laughed too loudly, who danced even when there was no music, whose presence lit up every room she walked in. And now she was here. Ready to vanish into dark water.

"Come down from there."

Her fingers loosened, but she didn't move.

"Let's go," he said again. "We'll go somewhere. Eat. Talk." His voice was unraveling, words getting smaller, slipping through the cracks of desperation.

And then, finally, she moved. Slowly, she turned, swinging her legs over to his side of the world. She climbed down and stood there, not looking at him, not speaking, just existing in the space he refused to let her leave.

He didn't say anything, just turned toward the car. She followed.

The cold was still there. But somehow, it didn't hurt anymore. Or maybe he had just gone numb.

2 | ELISEO

The silence was heavy.

Eliseo took her to the first place he saw open that late, which turned out to be a run-of-the-mill restaurant. It didn't look like it had good food, but he was desperate to go somewhere to break the tension. The place was nearly empty beside a few stragglers scattered around. They sat in a booth without words and looked over their menus.

"Know what you want?" he asked after a few minutes.

"Yeah," she spoke for the first time, her voice quiet.

Eliseo considered her for a moment before he took his jacket off and held it out to her. She looked at it, then at him, and hesitated, but eventually took it and slid it on. The waitress came shortly after. She gave them a smile that was more professional than warm, and introduced herself as Lacey. She asked if they were ready to order.

Juliana didn't even look at her. She barely moved. "I'll just have a small bowl of broccoli."

He raised his eyebrows. "That's it?"

She nodded like she didn't care. Like she *couldn't* care.

He sighed and looked at his own menu, but the words blurred. He didn't want anything, but he forced himself to pick something. "I'll have a cheeseburger and fries."

As Lacey wrote their order down, she gave Eliseo a lingering look that made him feel like she knew who he was. He quickly turned his head, hoping she didn't. He let out a light breath of relief when she collected the menus and disappeared.

Once they were alone again, he turned back to Juliana. She was staring out that window. "You could've ordered more, you know. It's my treat."

"I'm not hungry."

He stayed quiet for a moment, trying to find something to say. "So," he started, stumbling over his own words, "it's been ten years, right?"

She didn't answer right away. Just nodded.

He felt it then. The distance between them stretched out wider than he'd ever thought possible. She didn't want to talk. Didn't want to share. Didn't want to be there. Was it because of what just happened? Or was it because she didn't want to talk to *him*?

For a moment, Eliseo was seventeen again, stuck in the storm of her anger. He could see her in his mind – her eyes dark with unshed tears, her tight jaw, and her body shaking. Her anger was a hurricane, a force of nature, about to tear everything down around her. The foundations of their friendship crumbling in it.

"I don't want to see you ever again!"

The clatter of plates landing on the table jarred him from the memory. Lacey was back, her presence pulling him from a place he didn't want to be. How long had he been lost in his thoughts? He glanced at Juliana, her gaze fixed on her plate, a look of surprise flickering over her features. Had she been remembering too? Could they have been wrapped in the same past?

"Hey," Lacey broke the silence, her voice a little too eager. She turned to him, eyes curious. "Has anyone ever told you that you look like the guy who plays Justin Lee in *Bleed for the Badge*?"

He hesitated. "Yeah, that's me."

Her eyes widened, then narrowed, as if trying to place the pieces together. "It's you? You're actually him? Justin Lee? No way. What are you doing here in Tarver?"

"Visiting family."

Her gaze flicked to Juliana, seeking confirmation, but Juliana didn't even blink. Lacey must've come to the conclusion on her own, because she whipped out her notepad, all excitement now, her voice quick with disbelief. "Oh my gosh, I think I did read somewhere that you were from Tarver! Can I have your autograph, please?"

"Umm…"

"Please? I'm sorry I'm disturbing you two, but I love your show! I get together with my best friend Vanessa every Friday night to watch the new episode."

It was like a switch flipped. The moment someone saw Justin Lee in him, Eliseo De la Fuente stepped back. The change was quick, like slipping on an old, familiar coat. The version of himself the world wanted to see. A wide smile stretched across his face, and his posture laxed.

"Anything for a pretty face like yours." He winked at her, grabbing the pen with the same practiced ease and signing the pad.

She blushed, eyes wide with delight. "Thanks so much! Vanessa is going to freak out when I tell her you came here. She loves Justin!"

"And you? Do you love Justin?"

"He's charming, but way too reckless for me. My favorite character is Cassandra."

"Everybody says reckless until the plan works." He flashed her a grin, and he handed the pad back.

She squealed, too happy to be embarrassed. "Thank you again! Sorry for interrupting!" She gave Juliana a hasty apology and rushed back to work.

Eliseo turned back to Juliana to find that she was watching him. Her expression had shifted to disgust, irritation, and maybe even something deeper. Something he couldn't name, but he felt it. And underneath that gaze, Justin Lee disappeared. The shift back from Justin to Eliseo was never smooth; it was always accompanied with a drained feeling and shame. This time was no different. Just more intense.

Maybe it was the weight of remembering what had just happened – that she had been teetering on the edge of something darker and fatal, and here he was signing an autograph.

He looked down at his plate, avoiding her gaze. "I hope the food's good."

3 | JULIANA

Juliana thought the first ride had been as bad as it could get; her close friend from high school had just found her moments away from throwing herself off the Slade Tarver Bridge, after all. Their first reunion after ten years had been marred by the fact that he'd been the one to stop her from ending her life. How pathetic.

It had to be some sort of divine intervention. How had he just happened to be driving by at the very moment she was preparing to jump? When she turned to see Eliseo as the face behind the voice trying to convince her to rethink, she was frozen, caught between shock and an overwhelming sense of humiliation. The words wouldn't come, and she couldn't speak.

Why, of all people, did it have to be him?

She stayed silent through the whole ride. She thought it couldn't get any worse than that, but as the night dragged on, she realized she was wrong. The second ride, the one back to her house after the restaurant, was worse.

The moment they finished eating, she insisted he take her home. After she told him where she lived, the conversation fell away, as it had before. There were no directions to give; he'd been to her mother's house too many times to forget. So, once again, they were in silence. But this time, it wasn't just her embarrassment keeping her quiet. It was something else.

Ten years had passed since she last spoke to him. At first, she thought the pain was gone, that she was over everything. But after seeing him again, she saw that he wasn't the same Eliseo she remembered. It wasn't the same stabbing pain that cut deep like it had all those years ago. No, now it was more like a dull ache, a constant reminder, a persistent throb of an old wound, still not healed.

"So," he finally broke the silence as they stopped at a red light, "how's your mom and niece?"

"Fine," she answered flatly.

"Good." He hesitated, rubbing the back of his head, then tried again. "Anything new with them in the last ten years?"

"No."

"… okay."

That was it. That was all he said, and she thanked God for that. There was no more forced conversation after that. The quiet was almost a relief, even though it didn't quite erase the feeling of awkwardness between them.

They arrived at her house about fifteen minutes later. She opened the door to get out, but he stopped her.

"Wait," Eliseo said, his voice cracking.

She turned to him, already wary. His expression was troubled.

"What?"

He opened his mouth, then exhaled sharply, like he was gathering his thoughts. It didn't take her long to understand what he was struggling to say. She turned away, her voice quieter. "I'm not gonna do it again."

She could feel him watching her for a long moment. He was weighing her words, trying to decide if she was telling the truth. Finally, he let out a soft breath and faced forward again.

"… why do it at all?"

"We can't all be big-time actors living the dream," she muttered, an edge in her voice.

He seemed to be holding back, trying to find the right words. He sighed. "Juliana, it's been ten years. I know we didn't leave off on the best foot, and I know things have changed, but that doesn't mean I don't care. The last thing I want is to see you hurt or worse. Let me help you in whatever way I can."

She couldn't look at him. Instead, she kept her gaze fixed on her house. "You can help me by leaving."

There was no response at first. But then, those words from their last conversation rushed back to her.

"He was my best friend, Juliana. I knew him before I met you."

"So what? You're saying you were closer to him than me?"

"No. I'm saying that I understand your pain. I loved him too."

"Just leave."

"Don't do this."

"Get out of here, Eliseo, and don't come back."

"No."

For a few seconds, she wasn't sure whether those words had come from her memory or the Eliseo sitting next to her. But then she looked at him, his expression serious, and she knew.

"No," he repeated, his voice firm. "I'm not gonna leave, Juliana. You don't have to accept my help. You don't have to talk to me. You don't even have to acknowledge my presence. But you can't make me leave. Not again."

She stared at him. What was he trying to prove?

His face softened then, like he remembered where he was. "Look, I'm gonna be in town for a few weeks. We should talk. Catch up or something. I don't know…" He rubbed the back of his head again, awkwardly. "We don't have to, but it'd be nice, you know?"

That awkwardness, that fumbling uncertainty, hit her in a way she wasn't prepared for. It reminded her of the old Eliseo – the one who tripped over his words, who observed better than he communicated, and always cared. That was the Eliseo she remembered.

But this version of him wasn't that guy anymore. The person next to her was an impostor. He had Eliseo's face and voice, but everything else was different. This was the guy who'd charmed the waitress at the restaurant, the guy who had the confidence of a celebrity, and the guy who clearly didn't care.

Catch up? She scoffed silently. What was there to catch up on? She already knew everything.

She didn't answer him. Instead, she got out of the car and shut the door behind her. She didn't know what she was walking away from, but she did so without hesitation. She walked up the path to her front door.

The familiar weight of the flower pots at her feet reminded her of something she hadn't thought about in ages. She reached into the middle one, feeling around until she found the spare key hidden there. She'd told her mother a hundred times that it was a bad idea to keep the spare key so openly placed, but she never listened. Of course, tonight, she was glad she hadn't.

She closed the door softly behind her, locking it quietly, not wanting to disturb her mom or niece. She tiptoed up the stairs, stopping only when she heard light snores from their bedrooms. The quiet comfort of it was a stark contrast to the chaos in her mind.

Once she reached her room, she just stood there, in the dark, staring at nothing. Everything felt unreal. Less than two hours ago, she had been on that bridge, preparing to end it all. Now she was back there, in the same room, the same house, like nothing had ever changed… but had it changed?

She collapsed onto the bed, exhaustion sinking into her bones. As she laid there, she felt something crinkle underneath her. She reached beneath her and pulled out the letter she had written to her mother – the one that had been meant as her final goodbye. She held it for a moment before shoving it in the jacket pocket.

Was she really there? Did Eliseo De la Fuente really take her home? Did he really save her, or was she sinking in the water, dreaming all of this? And if it was a dream, why him? Why not someone else?

Why not Anthony?

4 | JULIANA

The sound of a fight and an all-too-familiar voice jolted Juliana out of her sleep. She stirred, still wrapped in the heaviness of the previous night. For a moment, she didn't open her eyes. She just breathed. Then the voice came again. Eliseo's voice.

"You've got secrets, I've got secrets. The real question is which one of us is better at keeping them?"

She groaned and cracked one eye open.

Bleed for the Badge.

The volume was too loud – the kind of loud that was intentional.

"Quince…"

Juliana sat up slowly. She swung her legs over the bed and sat there a moment, staring down at the hardwood floor. Her phone buzzed on the nightstand. She grabbed it. Three missed calls. A text from her mother asking her to come to the flower shop. She pressed the phone to her forehead with another groan.

Juliana usually worked from home, handling the flower shop's online orders, managing the website, and sorting deliveries. It was easier that way. No people. No questions. But when things got busy, her mom called her in. And today, of course, had to be one of those days.

She returned the text, saying that she'd be there in an hour. Not long ago, she'd been sitting on the side of the Slade Tarver Bridge, about to end her life. Not long ago, she saw Eliseo again. Not long ago, she was eating with him at some two-bit restaurant. It felt like a distant memory. She wanted to keep believing it was a dream, but his jacket around her said otherwise. She took it off and tossed it on the floor.

Juliana went downstairs, prepared to tell her fifteen-year-old niece to turn the volume down. She found her sitting on the couch with a defiant frown. The TV lit up the space with warm, flickering light. On the screen, Eliseo was grinning and his eyes were shining, looking like he was invincible.

Juliana stepped into the room, shooting her a knowing look and folding her arms. "Why do you have the volume so high?"

A pause. Then Quince turned it down. "You said you were gonna help me with volleyball drills in the morning. It's almost noon, and I've been up since forever."

Juliana sighed and put a hand on her head. She'd forgotten about that. Probably because she didn't think she'd be there to do so. "I'm sorry, I forgot. I'll make it up to you. Promise."

Quince cut her eyes at her. "You better. Tryouts are next month, and I want to be captain. How else am I gonna get Mark to notice me?"

"You could always try talking to him like a normal person. You don't have to like everything he likes."

"No offense, but your love life doesn't exactly make me want to listen to you."

Juliana smiled faintly despite herself. That was Quince – bold, ambitious, and full of opinions that no one asked for.

It started off as a temporary arrangement. Her older sister, Tessa, begged their mother for help raising Quince while she went to school. A few months turned into ten years, and Tessa was still "trying to find herself". Juliana used to be angry. Not just for herself and her mother, but for Quince.

Angry that her sister could leave a whole human being behind and sleep peacefully at night. But Quince never cried for her mother. Not once. She was weird like that. Strong like that. It seemed this family was too good at picking up after loss.

She glanced at the screen. Eliseo was eating food with his co-star. The same look on his face from yesterday. She grimaced. "Isn't there anything else on?"

"You know," Quince said, leaning back. "You're probably the only person I know who hates this show."

Juliana didn't respond.

Everyone loved it. The cast was everywhere – late-night interviews, magazine covers, TikTok edits. And at the center of it all: Eliseo.

Detectives Justin Lee and Cassandra Cherry go undercover as fighters to investigate a series of murders plaguing the underground fight scene. As they navigate this violent world, they must fight to survive, keep their cover intact, and uncover the truth behind the killings.

She only saw the first episode, and that was three years and three seasons ago. She had been so shocked to see him. Since when did he take up acting? He looked so different. In high school, his hair had been on the longer side, but now it was cut short in a variation of a fade. And he had facial hair. More shocking than that was that there wasn't a trace of social awkwardness. No, instead, he was cracking jokes, flashing brave grins, and fighting.

And that was the reason she never watched another episode. That was the reason she was disgusted with him at the restaurant. And that was the reason she wanted nothing to do with him. Not because of their last conversation in high school…

But because he was acting like Anthony.

And she hated it.

She hated the way people loved him for it. Watching him act like that, watching the world fall in love with a shadow of someone who was gone… felt like a cruel joke. Here she was barely surviving after the loss, and Eliseo was getting applauded for it.

"Yeah, well, bad actors," she muttered before walking out of the room.

5 | ELISEO

The smell of coffee drifted down the hallway, pulling Eliseo from a light sleep. He blinked against the morning light creeping through the blinds, and his ears adjusted to the Philippine music playing from downstairs.

Home.

He hadn't realized how much he missed the creak of these floors, the faded paint on his old bedroom walls, the distant hum of his parents moving around the kitchen like they always had – like time hadn't touched this place, even though it had taken everything else.

Eliseo pulled on a hoodie and made his way down the hall, where warmth, garlic rice, eggs, and laughter waited. His mother and father were sitting at the dining room table, talking and looking very much like they'd been married for thirty years. When they saw him, their eyes lit up in the way of proud parents.

"There he is," his father beamed. "Sleeping in like a TV star."

"Good morning," Eliseo said, smiling at both his parents.

"Look at you, still handsome as ever," his mother said, standing up to give him a hug. After, she stepped back and gave him an assessing look. "But thinner. Are you eating well? Have you been sleeping? Are you seeing anyone?"

Eliseo chuckled as he slid into a seat. "In that order? Sort of, not really, and no."

His father raised an eyebrow. "Still working that intense schedule?"

"Yeah, but I've got this break before filming starts up again."

"Well, I'm glad you're home for a little while," his mom said with a satisfied smile, fixing him a plate. "You can rest, eat good food, and maybe find someone to give me a grandchild?"

"Ma…"

"I'm just saying! You're my only child, and it's your responsibility. Besides, I want to see you happy." She paused, voice softening, "You've been working so hard and you've looked tired in the interviews lately…"

Eliseo said nothing at first. He felt it in his chest like a weight. Tired of pretending, of smiling on command, of being someone else on and off set. He thought the role would help him escape, but lately it felt like the thing he needed to run from most.

"I just needed to breathe for a while and figure some stuff out," he admitted softly. "Being back here helps."

"How long are you staying?"

"Two or three weeks."

He looked up and his eyes landed on the photo hanging by the archway – it was Anthony, forever seventeen. He was mid-laugh in the picture, one arm around Juliana, the other around Eliseo, all three of them sun-soaked and stupidly young. The sight of it punched Eliseo's chest before he could brace for it. His parents still never took it down. Probably never would.

"I saw Juliana yesterday," he said suddenly.

His mother looked up. "Juliana Ward?"

"Yeah. After I got my rental car and was on my way here."

"How is she?" his father asked. "We haven't seen her in… well, it's been about a year. Maybe longer."

The image of her on the bridge flashed in his mind. The panic. The cold. The silence. He didn't want to talk about that part yet. It wasn't his story to tell.

He looked down at his plate. "She's… different. Changed."

His mother was quiet for a moment, then nodded slowly. "A lot of time's passed. You've changed, too."

He didn't say anything at first. "You're right."

His father began to speak in Tagalog. Something that typically only happened when he was concerned. "Parang may bumabagabag sa'yo. Gusto mo bang pag-usapan?" *Seems like something's bothering you. Wanna talk about it?*

Eliseo shook his head.

"Kung nasasaktan ka, sabihin mo," his mom followed suit. *If you're hurting, tell us.*

She walked over and smoothed his hair like she used to when he was a kid. He loved his parents. They were everything good and grounding in his life. But even surrounded by warmth, he felt the chill creeping in again.

He hadn't wanted to admit how much he was drowning. How empty he felt pretending to be this character. How seeing Juliana somehow made him feel worse.

"I'm fine," he said finally, forcing a smile to his face. "Just figuring everything out."

6 | ELISEO

Eliseo adjusted his hat and face mask. He thought he wouldn't have to worry about being recognized back in his small hometown – he'd gone to great lengths to keep that information hidden from the public – but after the restaurant experience, he realized it still leaked out. So when his mother asked him to accompany her on some errands, he made sure to cover up.

He survived the two grocery stores; he kept his head down for the most part, only looking up when his mother needed help reading the label on unfamiliar brands. Now, they were headed across town to a flower shop to get a gift for his father's coworker.

"He's having a girl," his mom said, tapping her fingers against the steering wheel. "He's pretty nervous about it because he's used to boys. He has four of them. You remember Dr. Cavanaugh, right?"

"Yeah," Eliseo said, staring out the window at passing stores. "He always smelled like coffee and cigars."

His mom laughed. "That's the one."

They cruised down the street and turned the corner into a small lot tucked behind a bakery and nail salon. A painted sign over the front window read *Ward's Flowers & Gifts* in curling script, with little vines painted around the lettering. The glass windows were lined with potted plants, all bursting with color.

"Ward's…?" Eliseo murmured. "This place new?"

"It's actually Diane's shop."

His eyebrows hiked. "Juliana's mom?" He remembered her having a green thumb and talking about owning her own shop one day; he was happy to see she actually did it.

His mother parked and pulled her purse from the backseat. "When you said you saw Juliana, it reminded me of the shop. Let's go."

He hesitated. "I'll wait in the car."

"Come on, Diane would love to see you."

He couldn't deny her.

The bell above the flower shop door gave a soft jingle. Eliseo stepped inside, his hands stuffed in his coat pockets. The scent of lavender and rosemary hit him even through the mask.

The place looked nice – warm light, rustic shelves, vases in every shape, bouquets half-wrapped on the counter. A woman stood behind the counter, her presence quiet but unmistakable. Ms. Ward.

She must've been in her fifties, though the years had touched her gently. She was slender, almost delicate, with silver-streaked hair pulled back in a way that made her green eyes shine even brighter against her pale complexion.

He could see so much of Juliana in her. But where Ms. Ward was pale and her hair was straight, Juliana's complexion was a warm bronze, and her curls full and untamed. She stood taller, too – five-foot-ten, just like him. The contrast only made their similarities more striking. They both carried a kind of beauty that didn't ask for attention. It just was.

"Hello, welcome to Ward's–" Ms. Ward looked up with a gentle smile, and stopped when she saw them. "Jocelyn?" She wiped her hands on her apron and immediately went to hug her. "How are you? It's been a while."

"I know. It's been so long." She mirrored her smile as they embraced. "I've been meaning to drop by here and now I finally have a reason to…"

They chatted lightly until they suddenly remembered his presence. "And who is this?" Ms. Ward asked.

He pulled his hat back and moved the mask down. "Hey, Ms. Ward."

"Eliseo!" Ms. Ward's eyebrows shot up in disbelief. She pulled him into a hug. "How are you? The TV star graces us with his presence!" She gushed over him. "And so handsome! Look at that beard! Juliana, come out here!"

He laughed lightly until she called for Juliana. His smile faded. "Well, no, we don't have to…"

Juliana came out from the back, her hair was pulled back in a puff, arms deep in a mess of flowers. There was a single smudge of dirt on her cheek. She stopped short when she saw Eliseo. Their gazes met. But only for so long before Juliana looked away.

"Look who it is!" her mom continued enthusiastically.

"Hey," she said casually. "Long time no see."

"Yeah."

Ms. Ward fawned over him a little longer, asking him a few questions and sharing how happy she was to see him again. Afterward, she turned her attention fully to his mother, and they went off to find the right flowers for a gift.

Eliseo stood by awkwardly and glanced at Juliana. "I didn't know you worked here." He shifted, feeling like an intruder. "My mom just needed to pick up some flowers."

She nodded once, short and tight. He could hear her breathe deeply through her nose. She still didn't look at him. But then she set the bouquet down, pressing her palms against the wood of the counter like she needed grounding. "My mom doesn't know about last night. Don't say anything."

He didn't respond. She caught it.

"I told you I'm not gonna do it again."

"You scared me," he said quietly.

She looked away and spoke in a small voice, "You weren't supposed to be there."

"That doesn't make me feel any better."

"I don't owe you an explanation." She gave him a hard look. "Just… please. I made a mistake. It would crush her if she knew."

He hesitated. "Come over for dinner."

"What?"

"My mom is making a nice dinner tonight, and my dad is working late, so it'll be just us. You should come."

A long, brittle silence passed between them. Then she grabbed the bouquet she'd been working on and thrust it into a vase too hard, a few petals breaking off. It wasn't meant to be blackmail, but judging by her hardened look, he guessed she took it as such.

He didn't correct her.

"What time?"

"Six. Your mom and niece can come too."

She shook her head. "Just me."

"Okay."

And that was the end of their conversation.

7 | JULIANA

Juliana stood on the porch with Quince, who was practically buzzing with excitement, oblivious to the quiet storm behind Juliana's eyes. Juliana had been here a hundred times before, but it felt like another life. This time was different.

Eliseo opened the door. His smile was gentle and easy. She saw a flicker of relief across his face when he saw her.

Before he could say anything, Quince stepped forward.

"Eliseo De la Fuente, a.k.a. Justin Lee," she said with the self-assurance of a teenager who watched too many interviews. "I know you remember me, but that was when I was a kid, and I don't remember you, so I'm going to introduce myself. I'm Quince Ward. Fifteen years old. A student. I love rock music, roller coasters, pineapple pizza, and *Bleed for the Badge*. I hate fish, horror movies, and camping. I'm going to own my own chain of hotels one day. It'll be called 'HQ'. I hope you'll stay there."

Eliseo blinked, caught off guard, and then laughed. "Wow, you've really grown."

"Thank you. I drink my milk."

"I know I said just me, but Quince really wanted to come and I owed her a favor…" Juliana explained lightly. Her niece insisted this was the only way she could make it up to her for not helping her with volleyball.

"That's fine. The more the merrier." He stepped aside. "Come on in."

Quince walked in. Juliana handed Eliseo his jacket before following. She made a point to bring it so that there would be nothing in her house to remind her of him.

The scent hit her first – eggplants, garlic, something rich and slow-cooked. It wrapped around her like a memory. She remembered long ago evenings here, tucked into laughter and food and the warmth of Eliseo's family, back when life didn't feel like walking barefoot over broken glass.

Mrs. De la Fuente appeared in the doorway of the kitchen, apron tied around her waist, and her face glowing. "Juliana," she said, pulling her into a hug. "It's so good to see you again. And you brought your beautiful niece with you! I remember when you were small and dumping fruit cups over your head."

"But you can call me Quince."

She laughed and said something in her native tongue before embracing her as well. It had been a while since Juliana heard it. It sounded like an interesting language. Eliseo offered to teach her once when they were in high school, but she didn't have the patience to learn another language back then.

Dinner was a stew with meat and vegetables in some thick peanut sauce. It smelled really good. She always enjoyed his mother's traditional cooking; she would ask Eliseo to bring leftovers to lunch for her in high school.

Sheesh. This place was bringing back memories.

They sat down around the table while Mrs. De la Fuente made plates. Once done, they said grace and started eating. Juliana fell in love with the meal after the first bite.

"So Eliseo," Quince began immediately, "is it true you do all your own stunts?"

"Not all," he said, "but enough to keep my mom worried." He flashed a smile at his mother, to which she playfully hit him on the shoulder.

"What about the one where you fell off that building saving Cassandra?"

"I did that one."

"I knew it. That's so cool." She sighed dramatically. "Do you think you need a beautiful and talented fifteen-year-old sidekick? Because I'm so available."

"Quince," Juliana said.

"I'm just asking." Quince held her hands up innocently.

Eliseo chuckled, lifting his cup. "I'll let casting know."

Dinner flowed easier than Juliana expected. The food was incredible, the house warm, and the conversation effortless. Not that she had to talk much, but there were no awkward gaps of silence. It was afterward, when Quince was helping Eliseo's mom get the dessert, when Juliana found herself in the living room by herself with Eliseo.

A quiet moment passed between them. The kind that's not awkward, but heavy. Like both of them knew what was beneath it, but weren't sure who should reach for it first.

"She's a firecracker," Eliseo said, jutting his chin in Quince's direction.

"That's one word for her."

"Reminds me of you back then. Uninhibited."

She looked away. She didn't want to think about back then.

"So listen, I asked you to come so we could talk. I just want to make sure you're okay…"

She looked around. She didn't want to have this conversation. Her eyes froze on a framed picture on the archway. It was Anthony.

His eyes were still bright. Still alive. The corners of his smile crooked, mischievous – like he had just whispered a secret into her ear and dared her not to laugh.

Her breath caught.

And then everything unraveled.

The world tilted. The warmth drained from her limbs, replaced by a paralyzing cold that swelled from her core and pressed outward like a scream with nowhere to go.

The memory surged.

Tires shrieking. Steel twisting. Glass falling like rain. His name on her lips, swallowed by the impact. His blood, warm and shocking, on her hands as she held him.

She stumbled back. She needed air. Needed space. She ran to the front door.

Outside, the wind was cruel. It knifed through the trees, pushed against her skin like it wanted to remind her that she was alive – that she had survived. But that only made it worse.

Her breath was shallow, fast. Her lungs couldn't find rhythm. Her fingers curled into her sleeves like she was trying to disappear inside herself.

The cold didn't sting. Not compared to the memory.

She didn't want this. Not now. Not again.

She heard footsteps. She knew it was Eliseo before he even approached her. He didn't speak right away. She didn't look at him. This was the worst.

"Juliana," he said suddenly. Softly. "You're not alone. I'm here. Can you look at me?"

She didn't. Couldn't.

"That's okay, too. Just listen to me."

Her breathing was sharp and uneven.

"Breathe in with me," he said. He inhaled slowly, audibly, letting her hear the rhythm.

"And now out… just like that."

He repeated it. Again. And again.

Her shoulders twitched. Her breath hitched. But then the faintest echo of his rhythm in hers.

"That's good," he murmured. "You're doing really good. You're safe. Right here. With me."

His voice was the opposite of the chaos in her chest. It was solid ground.

"Count with me," he said. "Five things you can see."

She shook her head, tears slipping down her cheeks.

"Doesn't have to be perfect," he said. "Just try."

Her voice was broken, but she whispered, "A fire hydrant…"

"Good. What else?"

She blinked, eyes scanning. "Trees… cars…. your shoes…"

He smiled gently. "One more."

She hesitated and looked up at him. "You."

Eliseo's breath caught, just for a second. He put his jacket around her shoulders. Her breathing, still unsteady, began to slow.

"You're here," he said. "You made it through."

She began to cry. Not loud but deep. She leaned into him. He told her it was going to be alright as he held her.

And she believed him.

Not fully. Not forever.

But enough for that night.

8 | ELISEO

Eliseo lay on his back, staring at the ceiling. He exhaled through his nose, slowly.

The house was still. Too still. His parents had gone to bed hours ago, and the only sounds now were his occasional sighs. The dinner dishes were washed, the laughter from Quince long faded, and Juliana was gone.

Eliseo ran a hand over his face, pressing his palms against his eyes like he could push the regret back in. He thought inviting her to dinner was the right move. That maybe, just maybe, putting her back in a place where warmth still lived might ease something in her.

But he didn't know how much she was still drowning. He thought she was floating. Hurt, yes. Different, yes. But afloat. Then came the panic attack.

And Eliseo just stood there at first, stunned and slow like he hadn't spent the last few years pretending to be a man who had everything under control. He followed and helped her, eventually. But not fast enough. Not the way a friend should've. Regardless, he was grateful for the lessons the cast took for helping people with panic attacks. It was for an episode in the last season. At least something good came from the show.

He rolled onto his side, one arm curled under his head, and stared at the pale glow of his phone screen on the nightstand. He hadn't touched it in hours. Didn't want to.

The weight of the past crept in, slow and heavy. It always did at night.

He could still hear the crunch of metal. He could still see the blood gushing from his arm. The headlights had come from nowhere. A drunk driver ran a red light and turned everything upside down in the span of three seconds.

Juliana had been behind the wheel, Anthony in the passenger seat, and himself in the back.

He remembered yelling Anthony's name right before the car flipped. Remembered seeing him, for half a second, unbuckled, turning his head to look at Juliana. And then gone. Just like that. Through glass. Through air. Through life.

That was their senior year.

That was supposed to be their season of beginnings. College applications. Prom. Maybe a road trip. Instead, it was a funeral. Hospital rooms. Court dates. The sound of Anthony's mother sobbing down the hallway.

He hadn't slept right ever since.

And now... now he understood something deeper. He wasn't the only one lying awake in the dark. Juliana had been too. For years.

And he'd asked her to come. He'd *asked* her.

Eliseo swallowed hard and closed his eyes, trying not to picture the look on her face when the panic took her. Trying not to feel the guilt swimming in his ribs.

Tomorrow, he'd go to the flower shop and apologize. For pushing. For forgetting.

He owed her that much. And more. Because no one ever tells you that grief doesn't grow quieter with time. It just becomes part of the room.

And now, finally, he could see the shape of hers.

A match to his own.

9 | ELISEO

He walked into the flower shop with a teddy bear, a pair of gloves, and a box of chocolates. It was the only thing he could think of to apologize with.

Only her mother stood behind the register, her hair tucked into a scarf, her hands gently pruning a bouquet. He moved his hat and mask and offered a smile.

"Eliseo," she said, her voice soft with delight at seeing him again. "What are you doing here?"

"Hey, Ms. Ward. I was looking for Juliana. Is she here?"

"She's not. She only works in person if I'm in desperate need," she said, eying the things in his hand. "Are those for her?"

"Yeah." Eliseo bobbed his head. "I don't know if she or Quince told you, but they came over for dinner last night and it ended a little... rough."

She nodded. "She saw a picture of Anthony."

"I thought inviting her to dinner might be good. I thought we would catch up, but I didn't realize how much she was still carrying."

"You're not the only one who's a good actor, you know," she said after a long pause. "Juliana got really good at pretending she was okay. But a mask is still a mask no matter how long you wear it. At some point, it must come off."

Eliseo swallowed hard at that. For a moment, he didn't know what to say. She was talking about Juliana, and yet the words struck him. He shook it off.

The thought of what happened on the bridge resurfaced, and he considered telling her. He couldn't live with himself if something happened to Juliana and he didn't warn her mother. Maybe he wasn't the one to help her, but someone else could.

He sighed. "I think my being here triggers bad memories. I came to apologize and tell her I'll stay away."

Ms. Ward's expression shifted immediately. She came around the counter, wiping her hands on her apron. "Eliseo," she said, standing in front of him now, looking him square in the eyes. "You've always had a good heart. Even back then, when all three of you were thick as thieves, you had this… light. Like a lighthouse, guiding people to safety."

He said nothing.

"Juliana needs that light," Ms. Ward continued. "The accident didn't just take the boy she loved – it took her joy, her peace, and her faith. I watched the light go out of her eyes. And I tried to keep her above the waters…" Her gaze was distant. She reached out and placed a hand on his arm suddenly. "I know you're only here for a little while," she said. "But don't give up on her. Please."

Eliseo nodded slowly. He couldn't explain it, but he knew he needed to do this.

"I won't." His mouth responded before his mind could catch up.

"Good." She smiled then. "Why don't you come over for dinner tonight? You can give that to her yourself."

He blinked and hesitated.

"I'm making a chicken alfredo. You always liked my chicken alfredo."

Eliseo chuckled despite himself and nodded. "True. Okay, I'll come."

He left the flower shop with the scent of eucalyptus in his coat and a quiet resolve in his chest.

10 | JULIANA

In the morning, Juliana had sat on the edge of her bed for what felt like hours after waking. She didn't cry. She didn't move. She just breathed, shallow and slow, like something was broken inside of her and she was trying not to jostle the pieces.

The panic attack at Eliseo's place still clung to her. Every time she closed her eyes, she was back in that moment, his eyes wide and her chest heaving. She hated how undone she'd been. Hated that he'd seen her that way. Hated that part of her had found solace in his presence. Hated that she'd kept his jacket on like it was a lingering embrace.

But today was a new day, and eventually, Juliana found her footing. She pulled herself up, washed her face with cold water, and put her hair in two French braids. A quiet sort of strength bloomed. Just enough to keep moving through the day.

It was only after her mother returned from work that things took a turn. When she padded into the kitchen, the scent of chicken alfredo met her like a soft nudge, and she blinked at the sight of her mother bustling about, humming some hymn under her breath.

Juliana leaned against the doorframe, confused. "What's going on? Is Quince having someone over?"

Her mother didn't turn from the pan. "Hmm? No, honey."

"Then why are you setting the table like that?" Juliana's brow furrowed as she took in the extra plate, the folded cloth napkins, and matching glasses.

Her mother waved a hand, brushing the question away like a fly. "Don't worry about it."

After half an hour, the doorbell rang. That was when her mother called out, "Oh, sweetie, can you get that? It's Eliseo."

Juliana froze.

Eliseo. It repeated in her mind like a drumbeat. A mixture of emotions surged up – confusion, anger, and something like betrayal. Her breath stuttered in her chest, and her feet rooted to the floor.

But her mother kept humming, as if she hadn't just thrown a live grenade into Juliana's day. And something inside Juliana, brittle but stubborn, pushed her forward. She made herself move, her steps slow and careful, like walking across ice.

At the door, she hesitated. Took one long, grounding breath. She refused to let her hands shake as she reached for the handle.

When she opened the door, there he was. Standing there with his hands full of items and his eyes a little too gentle. She hated the way a part of her relaxed at the sight of him.

Juliana kept her face still, her voice even. "Hey."

"Hey."

Eliseo handed her the stuff in his hands immediately. She stared at it. A box of chocolates, a teddy bear, and gloves.

"It's for you. I came by the shop earlier to give it to you, but your mom said you weren't there."

"What for?" Pity. Because of the panic attack.

"I wanted to apologize."

She was caught off guard.

"I feel like yesterday was my fault because I pushed too hard. I was trying to help, but I ended up hurting you. I'm sorry."

She stared at him for a moment. She remembered the steadiness of his voice that night. The way he guided her through the storm of her own breath. The warmth of his jacket. The stillness of his chest as she wept into it.

"I'm not trying to aggravate you or get in your business." He hesitated. "I just… want to be here for you."

"Why?"

"Because I still care about you."

Silence. She studied him then. There was something in his gaze – not the kind of softness that came from pity, but the kind born from understanding.

Her voice cracked a little, but she didn't care. "So my mom invited you over for dinner?"

"Yeah. She promised to make chicken alfredo, and I couldn't refuse."

Before she could say something else, Quince popped into the room like a bolt of chaos.

"There he is! Our favorite actor! I'm so glad you're here!" She pointed at him dramatically, eyes gleaming. "Do you know how many kids at school I texted about our dinner? They want proof. We have to get a picture this time."

Juliana let out a quiet sigh as she took the stuff upstairs to her room. She laid the items gently on her bed, fingers brushing the edge of the gloves.

He must've noticed that she hadn't worn any. But it was the color that gave her pause. Baby blue. Her favorite color. The one she'd had her room painted with since she first saw it as a kid. Ten years later, and somehow, he still remembered. Something twisted and softened in her chest at the same time.

She made her way back down to the kitchen, where everyone was seated. Of course, the only empty seat was next to Eliseo. When she sat down at the table, they said grace and started eating.

She didn't have to talk because once again, Quince talked endlessly. "So are you rich now? Like do you own a mansion or something?"

Eliseo laughed. "Not a mansion. I rent a small place. L.A. prices are crazy."

"Do you have a pool?"

"Yes."

"A butler?"

"No."

"Are you dating Cassandra in real life? I know you guys are dating in the show, but she posted a heart emoji under your photo last month so…"

Eliseo blinked, clearly caught off guard. "No, I'm not dating her. Or anyone. I'm single."

"So is Juliana," Quince said, glancing at Juliana, "for, like, the past five years."

Juliana nearly dropped her fork. "Quince."

"What? I'm just connecting dots. Like a good niece. You two were friends before anyway…"

"That's enough, Quince." Her mom shot Quince a look, although it was accompanied with an amused smile.

"You'll have to excuse her, Eliseo. She's fifteen and doesn't understand the art of subtlety yet."

"Yeah, I picked that up yesterday." He laughed lightly as he rubbed the back of his head.

Juliana felt her cheeks heat up, and she kept her gaze on her plate. She hated the embarrassment filling her chest and the growing awkward atmosphere. Thankfully, her mother carried most of the conversation after that, chattering about the weather, church, and how the neighbor's son had gotten into college. The kind of talk that floats above the deeper things.

When dinner ended, Quince groaned as she was given dish duty, and Juliana's mother murmured an apology before stepping away to take a call. The two of them sat there for a moment before Eliseo rose, saying it was getting late. As he started toward the front door, Juliana followed him. But something in her – something older than the grief – didn't want him to leave yet. She glanced toward the living room, then back at him. She reached for the casual tone that had saved her in so many conversations before.

"If you're not in a rush," she said lightly, before he could say goodbye, "I was gonna put on a movie."

Eliseo looked at her. Surprised, at first, but it simmered to something akin to appreciation. "I'm not in a rush."

They sat on opposite ends of the couch, a safe distance apart. Not because they were afraid of each other, but because grief still sat in the room with them, even now.

When he took his cardigan off to get comfortable, her eyes immediately went to the long scar on his forearm. A result of the accident. She traced it with her eyes, looked down, and then turned back to the television. Yes, grief still sat between them.

She turned the channel, and the movie began to flicker across the screen. It was the comedic kind they used to put on during late summer nights, when Anthony would fall asleep halfway through and she and Eliseo would still be quoting lines long after the credits rolled.

It wasn't the same. Of course it wasn't.

But it was comfortable.

And that counted for something.

Halfway through, Juliana spoke, her voice low, "How did you know to do that? When I was having a panic attack."

"One of the side characters on the show has panic attacks, so the cast had to learn proper techniques like that for a few episodes last season."

She nodded and didn't say anything else.

Eventually, Eliseo spoke again. "You remember in high school, when you used to make me read the school books out loud to you?"

She smiled without looking at him. "You read better than I did."

"You didn't even try."

"Yeah," she said, leaning her head back against the couch cushion. "But your voice was… soothing. It made things make sense. I could barely be still back then, but when you read, I couldn't move."

Eliseo didn't answer right away.

He reached toward the small side table and grabbed the nearest book – a Bible, worn and soft from years of use. Her mother's Bible.

He looked at her. She didn't stop him.

He opened it to the page marked and began to read.

"For God so loved the world that He gave His only begotten Son, that whoever believes in Him should not perish but have everlasting life. For God did not send His Son into the world to condemn the world, but that the world through Him might be saved."

The room hushed.

Not out of tension. Maybe out of reverence.

Juliana stared at the television, but she wasn't watching anymore. And for a moment, she could feel another presence sitting on the couch between them. Something other than grief.

11 | ELISEO

Juliana slept like someone with too many things on her mind. She had curled into herself on the couch, her head resting against the armrest, one hand tucked beneath her cheek. The soft hum of the muted television flickered across her face, coloring her in shifting blues and golds. Across from her, Eliseo sat in the same place he'd been all night, his body stiff and his thoughts restless.

He hadn't expected her to ask him to stay.

They had spoken over dinner, sure, but nothing profound had been said — nothing that would've softened her heart toward him. Just the polite, careful dance of two people who knew a secret. If anything, he thought Quince's antics would've furthered the gap between them because of the awkwardness. But something must've changed between the first forkful of food and the last sip of water. Maybe a truce that neither of them named.

He let his head fall back against the couch, exhaling as he stared up at the ceiling. He thought about the scriptures he had read earlier.

He and Anthony had read those verses together before. Sat side by side as he explained to him what it meant. He was the one who'd led Anthony to Christ, but after he died, he couldn't read the Bible anymore. Couldn't touch the pages without feeling like it had betrayed him. But sitting there with Juliana made it a little easier.

He pulled his phone from his pocket, the screen lighting up with the time. Midnight. Seven missed calls from his mother. And then there were a few messages from Sophia, who'd checked in earlier, asking how the vacation was going.

True enough, they had gone out a handful of times, enough to test the waters, but they found that friendship suited them better. In a way, they understood each other more than most could. Both had faced the same quiet problem: people liked the character they played on TV more than them.

Every woman he had ever dated had been drawn to the version of him they saw on-screen – the confident, charming rebel with a well-timed one-liner. It was exhausting pretending to be someone else. With Juliana, at least, he didn't need to play a part. He could just be himself.

She was the girl who excelled in volleyball, spoke her mind, and whose presence gave people permission to be themselves. He was the guy who was quiet and smart, and made sure she didn't forget her umbrella, and who brought her some of his mother's cooking for lunch. Back then, he thought maybe she could see him the way he saw her. But he quickly learned that she liked Anthony. And why wouldn't she? Anthony was the fun and exciting one. Something about him was electric and attractive – everybody loved him.

Sheesh. This place was bringing back memories.

The screen flickered, shifting his reflection into the familiar face of someone he no longer wanted to be. Justin Lee. A commercial for *Bleed for the Badge*.

It was like a trap door opened beneath him.

A wave of pretending swelled over his head, choking him and dragging him under. His heart pounded against his ribs like it wanted out. Ms. Ward's words from before echoed in his mind.

"God… you saved Juliana from drowning. Save me, too," he murmured.

With that, he pushed himself up to standing, his body suddenly feeling too heavy for the moment. He turned to leave but hesitated, looking back at Juliana one last time.

Her chest rose and fell in a slow, steady rhythm. He didn't want to leave. Especially since he didn't know if he'd ever get a moment like this again.

He finally turned and was startled by Quince. She was leaning against the frame, arms folded, face set in an unimpressed expression. She studied him for a moment.

"You're really not like him," she said finally. "Justin would've snuck a kiss or something."

He blinked. "That's… illegal?"

She shrugged. "Morally wrong, at best." Then she tipped her chin toward Juliana. "But I guess it's a good thing you're not like him. She hates Justin Lee. So maybe Eliseo De la Fuente has a chance."

Something in his chest tightened. He opened his mouth, then closed it again, uncertain of what to say. Finally, he just nodded, backing toward the door. His fingers found the handle.

"I was a kid when you two went to school together, so I don't remember how your relationship was, but I know this: if you play your cards right, it can be more than before."

"Um… goodnight, Quince."

She watched him with knowing eyes as he stepped out into the night.

What a strange evening.

12 | JULIANA

Juliana drove in silence.

The hum of the engine was soft beneath her fingertips, and the city rolled out ahead of her like a familiar song she hadn't heard in a while. She adjusted the rearview mirror, catching a glimpse of Quince in the back seat, earbuds in, nodding her head to music Juliana couldn't hear. The mall was only fifteen minutes away, and Juliana was tasked with dropping Quince off.

She'd gotten good at driving again.

It had taken time – years, not months. The thought of being behind the wheel used to make her palms sweat and her throat close. Her body would flash back to the moment she saw headlights where they weren't supposed to be. The moment the world split into before and after.

But today she drove. Calm. Present. A victory, in its own quiet way.

"Text me when you're done," she said when Quince hopped out to join her group of friends.

Quince turned to her. "See if you can get Eliseo to come with you to pick me up. It'll be good for both of us."

Juliana rolled her eyes. "Bye, Quince."

She pulled off, turning toward the shop. A few deliveries waited; three small bouquets, each wrapped in brown paper and tied with satin ribbon. Something about driving them out herself every now and then, handing flowers to strangers, and watching their faces soften… it made the day feel less hollow.

The first two deliveries were uneventful. A birthday bouquet. An anniversary surprise. Kind people with open doors and brief words of gratitude.

At a red light, Juliana found her thoughts wandering back to the last evening. Watching the movie with Eliseo. Them sitting together like they did in high school. The way his voice wrapped around scripture like it was something sacred and still alive.

She'd watched him out of the corner of her eye while he read, his thumb rubbing the edge of the page like he was trying to hold something steady.

Eliseo had always had that steadiness in him. Back then, when Anthony was loud and wild and full of chaos, Eliseo was quieter. Gentle. He'd always been watching, always listening, and always caring.

She thought about the scar on his arm. She walked away unscathed on the outside, but Eliseo's arm was severely cut. It healed over time, but the memory was still there. Somehow, that didn't trigger a panic attack.

She hadn't made things easy for him since he came back. She knew that. Every wall she'd built, every cold shoulder, every harsh word – it was all anger. But he stayed.

That meant something.

She didn't want to admit it, but part of her wanted to be known by someone again. And Eliseo had known her once. Maybe not the same her that existed now, but enough.

Juliana breathed. Next time she saw him, she'd be softer.

Not open. Not yet. But kinder.

She turned the corner toward her last stop, a small house on Cedar and Plymouth. As she pulled up to a stop sign, a murmur of noise caught her attention. There was a gathering up ahead, near a café with large glass windows and patio seating. A small crowd had formed on the sidewalk, laughing and phone cameras flashing.

Juliana's breath slowed. Her fingers gripped the wheel as she realized what was happening. At the center of that crowd was Eliseo.

Young women, mostly teenagers and early twenty-somethings with eager eyes and phones held high. He was smiling, oozing a charm that disarmed those around him. He signed autographs, posed for selfies, touched a shoulder here, offered a wink there…

He didn't see her.

And just like that, the warmth she'd been feeling evaporated. The resentment surged before she could stop it. Fast and cruel.

He got where he was by pretending to be Anthony. The people out there didn't know that it was Anthony they really loved. Instead, they thought it was Eliseo. The pretender. She remembered why she was so against him.

Her foot slammed the gas once the coast was clear, tires squealing slightly as she turned the corner too fast.

She didn't look back.

13 | ELISEO

"Okay, so seriously," Sophia said, smooth and teasing. "Are you still alive out there in Gerber? I had to call and check. I was starting to think you'd run off into the woods or something."

Eliseo chuckled, the sound low and tired. "It's Tarver, and yeah, I'm still here. The cold is fierce, but not enough to send me packing… yet."

She laughed, that bright, familiar sound that had become a small comfort over the years. Sophia Kyle. On set, she played Cassandra, the steady, tender presence his character leaned on more than he ever admitted. In real life, she was a whirlwind of humor and heart. And for the past three seasons, someone he leaned on for support, too.

"You had me wondering," she said. "But how's vacation treating our favorite wise-cracking hero?"

He leaned back into the worn cushions, eyes tracing the shadows playing on the ceiling. "It's quiet," he said. "Feels like I actually have space to breathe out here."

"Good. You needed it. You weren't acting like yourself."

"I wasn't feeling like myself." A breath left him, long and uneven. "It's only been a few days, but things have already been… interesting."

"Interesting how?"

"I caught up with an old friend. It's been grounding."

There was a beat of silence on the line. Then, with a knowing lilt, "A friend, huh? Let me guess… a woman?"

"Yeah." His voice was softer now. "Juliana. We were friends back in high school."

"Dating the hometown girl." Sophia made a soft clicking sound with her tongue. "The media is gonna eat that up."

"It's not like that," Eliseo said, a little too quickly. "We're just friends."

"Is she single?"

"Yes, but—"

"Is she attractive?"

"That's not the point."

"Were you with her when I called?"

His silence spoke for him.

She laughed. "I may leak this to the press myself."

"Sophia…"

"I'm kidding, I'm kidding," she said and paused. "But seriously, I'm glad you've got someone there that's helping you recover. You need someone who can remind you who you are underneath all the noise. We all do."

A knot loosened in his chest.

There was a softer edge to her voice. "I've seen this business chew up better people than you so take your time. We don't start recording for season four until next month. Stay home a little longer if you need to."

He breathed. She was right. "You always know what to say… at least, when you're not threatening scandal."

"Comes with working on a melodramatic action show. We have the best one-liners."

He chuckled under his breath. "Thanks. Really."

"Take care of yourself, Eliseo."

They hung up. Eliseo let the phone fall to his side, his gaze returning to the ceiling. He was sprawled across the couch, the TV humming quietly in the background.

His parents were out, and he was bored. Earlier that afternoon, a crowd had gathered around him during a quick coffee run – a mess of his own making. He was still riding the ease of those hours with Juliana, the rare comfort of simply being himself. It had felt so natural, so good, that he'd forgotten to pull up his mask. A simple mistake. And he was quickly figured out.

He shifted into Justin Lee as always. He smiled. He took pictures. He flirted. He answered questions in that practiced, effortless tone.

But on the inside?

He was empty.

Drowning.

What started as an escape, a role that gave him purpose, now felt like it had swallowed him whole. The charisma. The humor. The quiet confidence. All borrowed pieces of someone who wasn't coming back.

Eliseo ran a hand over his face, breathing out slowly. He looked across the room and stopped at the sight of his father's Bible on the coffee table. He stared at it for a long time. He remembered how the words from reading with Juliana had settled in the silence.

He considered reading it again. He never stopped believing, but God didn't feel close anymore. He hadn't for a long time.

Eliseo had found acting after graduation, mostly by accident. Some general education class in college, and the professor had said he had "presence." For once, he didn't feel invisible, and he had a distraction from the pain.

So he kept doing it.

And when the role of Justin Lee came along, it was like stepping into a memory – an echo of Anthony. He could bring him back, in a way. Keep him alive in the smiles and the swagger.

It was comforting. Until it wasn't. Until the lines between them blurred, and he felt drained. Until it wasn't a distraction from the pain anymore but an amplifier.

Eliseo swallowed hard as he stared at the Bible.

He missed peace.

He missed being himself.

He missed Anthony.

And, quietly, he missed Juliana.

He exhaled deeply. He still wasn't sure how to move forward… but he knew Juliana was a part of the answer. Maybe the pull he felt toward her was not just for her, but for him, too.

14 | ELISEO

Eliseo's hands were in his pockets as he stood on Juliana's porch, a quiet wind lifting the hem of his coat. He knocked once, then again, lighter the second time. When it opened, Juliana stood in the frame with an expression reminiscent of how she looked at him when they were at the restaurant. It startled him, and he shivered involuntarily.

He moved his mask down. "Hey, Juliana."

She didn't say anything at first. Just looked at him. Her voice was low. "What do you want?"

He faltered. "I, uh, was just in the neighborhood. Thought maybe you'd wanna hang out for a bit. Talk. Walk. Whatever." He tried for a small smile. "I don't have your number, otherwise I would've texted."

Nothing. She leaned her shoulder against the doorframe like it took effort to stay standing in front of him. "No."

The single syllable fell like a stone into a deep well. Eliseo's brow furrowed. "Did I… do something?"

Her jaw tightened. Her gaze flickered down the street, then back at him, sharp as cut glass. "Yes. You came back here."

He was startled again.

"I saw you downtown with all your fans," she snapped. "Smiling and laughing, putting on that same charming act." She shook her head. "Just tell me, is it easy to play Anthony? Were you always planning to wear him like a costume?"

He stepped back, as if she just slapped him. "…what?"

Her arms crossed over her chest. "You walk around pretending to be someone who died. You get paid to wear his face, and you wonder why I don't want to be around you."

He struggled to find his words. His throat tightened. "Juliana– "

"Why are you here?" Her voice cracked on the last word.

A beat of silence stretched between them.

Eliseo exhaled, pain rising in his chest. "I'm trying… I'm trying to figure myself out. I never meant to be Anthony. This role… this life… it's been a lot."

"I can tell. The way you play it up on camera and off camera really says you're struggling."

"You think I'm happy like this? I feel I'm drowning in this role. I barely know who I am anymore. I can't even sleep at night."

"Poor Eliseo. He's got an apartment in L.A. with a pool and a million fans. It sounds tough."

Eliseo's pain sharpened into anger at that. He looked away, jaw clenched. He hated how she was making it seem like she was the only one who had lost someone important to them. Like she was the only one hurting. There was an edge in his voice. "I was in that car too, Juliana."

"Yeah, but you walked away."

"I *limped* away," he snapped. "And haven't stopped limping since."

They both stood in the stillness that followed. Grief vibrated in the air like a struck chord.

"You're not the only one grieving, Juliana! That was your problem back then!" he yelled, his frustration growing. "I was hurting too, and when I tried to be around the one person who could understand my pain, you pushed me away! You said you never wanted to see me again! I didn't just lose Anthony that day; I lost both of my best friends. And I had to figure out a way to deal with–"

He stopped suddenly when his vision blurred, and he turned away. He didn't know where he was going. He only knew he didn't want to be where she was right then. He didn't want her to see how much it hurt him.

He got in his car and drove off. His hands gripped the wheel tighter than necessary as he sped down the streets. Eventually, he found himself at the Tarver Cemetery.

The graveyard was quiet. Winter had stripped the trees bare, and the sky was that dull gray that didn't promise snow, but just left you guessing. There was no one else around. Just Eliseo, the gravestone, and everything unsaid.

He swallowed, staring at the chiseled name.

Anthony Minchella.

Eliseo let out a breath through his nose, sharp and uneven. "I know he's not here. I don't even know why I'm here."

His jaw clenched after a long minute.

"I didn't ask for any of it," he said suddenly, eyes flicking upward. "I didn't ask for this grief or this guilt."

His voice rose before he could stop it.

"You took him," Eliseo hissed. "He was the one everyone loved. He was like a brother to me. He wasn't perfect, we all know – he was reckless and he did stupid things, but he could've lived. He accepted You. He told me he was gonna marry Juliana one day. He was gonna change… he was gonna be good. And You took him and left me. Why?"

The wind howled gently across the open space.

Eliseo pressed his lips together and looked away, trying to hold it in, trying to be composed. But the tears were already burning. His shoulders began to tremble, fingers twitching at his sides. He scrubbed at his face with one hand, breath catching.

"I don't even know who I am anymore. And You–" He exhaled hard. "You feel so far. Like You dropped me in the middle of this grief and then just walked off."

He stared at the headstone again.

"I'm trying. I really am. But I don't know what to do."

Eliseo sank into a crouching position, the cold biting through the denim of his jeans. His breath came out in clouds. He didn't know what to say. The wind picked up, rustling the dead leaves. The silence pressed in.

Eliseo wiped his eyes roughly. Finally, he spoke, "I miss you, man…"

15 | JULIANA

Juliana sat on the edge of her bed, staring at her hands like they might explain why her heart was harder than it should've been. She felt like she knew why before, but now? Not so much. The fight with Eliseo was still pulsing through her like static, the words echoing with too much heat, too little grace.

She hadn't expected to see that look in his eyes. It wasn't arrogance like she thought it would be. It was something deeper. Betrayal. Sadness. Grief. Eliseo had looked like someone who hadn't let himself cry in years. And that's what got to her.

She sank back onto the bed. The ceiling above her blurred with thought. She remembered the way everything felt too loud the day after the funeral, and even a week after the funeral.

She'd stayed in her room with the blinds drawn, lights off, covers pulled over her head like maybe the darkness would swallow her whole and let her disappear.

Eliseo had called every day, but she couldn't answer. Seeing his name on the screen was like a gut punch – a reminder of everything that happened. She didn't need reminders. A car ride was a reminder. A hospital was a reminder. The pictures of Anthony in her phone were reminders. She wanted something that would comfort her. Eliseo couldn't do that for her this time... but he kept trying.

Her mom knocked gently on her door. "Juliana? Eliseo's here."

Juliana's heart sank. "Tell him to go away."

But he didn't. Of course he didn't. A minute later, there was another knock.

"Juliana?" he called softly.

She sat up slowly, arms wrapped around her knees. She didn't say anything.

The door creaked open, and there he was. Eliseo. Long hair a mess, eyes tired, face bruised. He looked like he hadn't slept either. For a second, her heart squeezed, and she wanted to hug him. But then her gaze fixed on his arm sling, and her own hurt bubbled up to the surface. She walked away with minimal damage – at least, externally. All of her wounds were on the inside.

"I just wanted to check on you," he said.

She didn't respond and turned away.

"It's gonna be okay."

"Okay? How can you say that? Nothing is okay, Eliseo."

He breathed and took a step closer. "It's not right now, but it will be."

She shook her head, eyes welling up. "Things can never be okay again. It was almost his birthday, he was almost eighteen… almost eighteen-year-olds aren't supposed to die. Everything hurts, and I don't know how to make it stop. I can barely look at you without falling apart."

"I know, but I'll be here for you."

"I just want to be alone."

"You've been alone for the past week. We should be close in a time like this. We need each other." There was a desperation in his voice. "He was my best friend, Juliana. I knew him before I met you."

"So what? You're saying you were closer to him than me?"

"No. I'm saying that I understand your pain. I loved him too."

"Just leave."

"Don't do this."

"Get out of here, Eliseo, and don't come back."

He just stared at her as if pleading with her not to make him leave. She had to say something to make him go… she just didn't expect it to come out so angrily.

"I don't want to see you ever again!"

He stood there, stunned and hurt, as if she'd just slapped him across the face. It took him a moment to pull himself together, and then he turned and walked out.

Back then, she thought he was implying that her grief wasn't as valid as his, but looking back, she could see that he was actually reaching out for help too. She needed to escape, but he needed to be embraced. Neither of them got what they were looking for, and it seemed the scars from that didn't heal quite properly.

There was a sudden soft knock on her door. She looked at the door and sat up, involuntarily calling out Eliseo's name.

"No, it's me," her mother said, walking in, holding a basket of folded laundry. She placed the clothes on the dresser and turned, eyes full of knowing. "Hoping for Eliseo, were you?"

"… no."

"You've been quiet," she noted, gently. "Everything alright?"

Juliana hesitated. "I said some things earlier to Eliseo. I think I was too harsh."

Her mother nodded slowly, not surprised.

"I just… I thought he was pretending. I thought he didn't take anything seriously." Juliana's voice broke slightly. "But when I said it, he got upset."

Her mother walked over and sat beside her, their shoulders touching.

"Honey," she said, "I told you a long time ago that you're not angry with Eliseo. You miss him. And he missed you. But there's a lot of hurt you two have to work your way through. It was bad enough to lose Anthony through death, but losing someone close to you who's still alive hurts differently. I learned that after your father left."

Juliana blinked, a lump forming in her throat.

Her mother turned toward her then, face calm and full of wisdom in the way women are after they've lost people and still learned how to sing afterward.

"You know, you're still working your way through grief, but at least you get to do so with people who understand and are patient with you. Eliseo lives in L.A. by himself with cameras all around. He has to hide his grief the best he can."

Juliana stayed quiet. She never thought about it from that perspective.

Her mother reached out and took her hand. "Sometimes the Lord brings people back into our lives for a reason. I believe Eliseo needs you just as much as you need him."

Juliana nodded slowly, tears pressing behind her eyes. She had been so caught up in her own ache, in the weight of her memories, that she hadn't seen his.

She decided quietly that she would go see him soon.

16 | JULIANA

Juliana stood on the small porch, wringing her hands, the cold air curling around her fingers.

Two days.

It had been two days since the fight.

Now, standing here, her heart felt like it might bruise itself against her ribs.

The door opened with a soft creak, and there stood Mrs. De la Fuente, her face brightening the moment she saw Juliana. Without hesitation, she reached forward, wrapping her in a warm, familiar hug. The scent of jasmine and kitchen spices clung to her sweater.

She murmured something gentle in Tagalog.

Caught off guard, Juliana leaned into the embrace, letting it steady her for a moment. "Hi, Mrs. De la Fuente. I'm sorry to drop by unannounced like this. I was hoping to talk to Eliseo. Just for a few minutes."

"Come in, come in."

She stepped into the warmth and let the door close behind her. His mother looked full of concern. "I'm glad you're here. Eliseo is upstairs. He hasn't come out except to use the bathroom. Something's wrong, but he won't talk to us. Maybe you can help him."

Juliana gave a soft, guilty nod. "I can try."

She swallowed hard. She climbed the stairs slowly. The hallway was quiet except for the distant murmur of the radio playing a Tagalog song downstairs. When she reached his door, she stood there for a moment, hand hovering near the knob.

She knocked gently. "Eliseo?"

Silence.

She waited, listening. A soft shift inside.

"I'm sorry," she said finally. Her voice was barely above a whisper, but the hallway caught it, echoed it back to her like a confession. "I shouldn't have said those things. I was angry, but you were right. I never thought about how you felt."

Still no answer.

"When I first saw you on TV, I was mad because I thought you moved on. I was struggling, and you looked like you were doing just fine. Then, when I saw how you were acting, I was angrier because I thought you got by pretending to be like Anthony." She swallowed hard. "I never realized you were struggling just as much as me – that you always had been."

A long pause.

She leaned closer to the door and laid a hand against it. "When I had my panic attack, you didn't leave. You stayed with me." She continued, "You said you feel like you can't breathe? I'm staying with you. Tell me five things you can see."

A few seconds passed. "The wall."

"What else?"

"The bookshelf… my suitcase… my sneakers…"

"Good. One more thing."

There was another long pause, and then, the door creaked open. Just a few inches.

His eyes met hers.

They were tired.

"You." With that, he walked over to his bed and sat at the edge of it. He hunched slightly, elbows on his knees, staring at the floor. The room was dim, and the afternoon sun filtered through half-closed blinds.

Juliana didn't say anything at first. She didn't ask him to talk or press him with questions. She just closed the door behind her and sat down beside him, her hands folded in her lap.

A few minutes passed like that. Her gaze wandered the room. It was tidy, but lived-in. Eliseo was always organized like that. Apparently, even in his sorrow. Her eyes drifted downward and caught the edge of something tucked beneath the bed frame. She knelt and pulled out a Bible. Eliseo didn't react, but she saw the way his shoulders stilled when she opened it.

She didn't know where to start. She had no plan. No sermon in her mouth. All she knew was that this was what her mother did for her many times. So she let the pages fall where they may, and began reading aloud. Eliseo shifted beside her, eyes still low.

Juliana read for a few minutes until she came to a scripture that made her stop. "He heals the brokenhearted and binds up their wounds."

Silence.

Then, without thinking too hard, she reached over and laid her hand gently on his arm. She took a breath and closed her eyes.

"God," she began, voice unsteady. "I don't know the right words, and I'm not as good at this as my mom is. But You know Eliseo. You know what he's carrying. You know what he's trying so hard to hold together. So I just ask that You meet him in the places where he's tired and remind him he's not alone. Remind him that You still see him. That You still love him. And help me to love him, too. And please forgive me for being so tough on him. I was wrong."

She opened her eyes, and then she saw it. The tears sliding silently down Eliseo's cheeks. He didn't wipe them away. He just let them fall, like they'd been waiting years to be seen.

She just reached for his hand and held it in both of hers.

"I'm so sorry, Eliseo."

17 | ELISEO

The local bowling alley didn't look like much from the outside – faded signage, a cracked sidewalk out front, and a flickering neon sign. But inside, it was clean, cozy, and mostly empty. A few older couples played quietly near the back. A mom wrangled her toddler in the arcade area. Other than that, it was theirs.

Juliana had insisted on it. After an emotionally draining morning, she knew they needed to do something to get their minds off the heaviness and break the previous tension.

Eliseo had raised a brow, skeptical. "Bowling?"

"Why not?" She was already heading downstairs before he could answer.

Now, a half hour later, they were lacing up ugly shoes and taking in the glow of red-and-blue lights that danced across the lanes.

"Take the mask and hat off," Juliana said, stepping into his line of sight. "I don't want any excuses when I beat you."

Eliseo laughed once, but hesitated, concerned about potentially drawing a crowd again. "I'll just keep it on."

"This place doesn't get a lot of business throughout the week. You can just be Eliseo here, I promise."

He still wasn't sure, but Juliana grabbed the hat off his head as if to make her point clear. He started to protest, but when he saw her smile, something in him relaxed, and he trusted her. He smiled back as he took his mask off.

Their first round was a mess. Eliseo overthrew his first two balls, and Juliana bowled straight into the gutter. But with each laugh, each playful shove of shoulders and exaggerated victory dances, something in the air lightened. By round three, Juliana was beating him by ten points and very much enjoying it.

"Don't look at me like that," he said, laughing as she struck a proud pose after another spare.

"Like what?" she teased.

"Like you just won the Olympics."

"Well, maybe I did. You don't know my life."

He opened his mouth to respond, a grin already tugging at the corner, but before a word could leave him, her foot caught awkwardly on the edge of the slick floor. She stumbled forward with a small gasp.

Eliseo reacted on instinct, lunging to catch her. His grip found her arms and pulled her upright before she could fall.

"You okay? That's not something I'd expect from someone who won the Olympics," he said softly, half-smiling.

She steadied herself. "Well… even champions stumble."

He held onto her arms a second too long. Their eyes locked. The moment breathed. When he finally let go, it was slow. They turned back to the game, but the air between them buzzed differently. His heart was pounding, but he tried to ignore it.

Juliana smoothed her shirt and cleared her throat like she needed to break the spell. "You know if I beat you, you owe me ice cream."

"And if I win?"

"Still ice cream, but I'll let you pick the flavor."

He laughed. He didn't know what this was between them, not yet. But it was something. A beginning or a mending. Something that made him forget everything else. Even if only for a little while.

Eventually, the bowling alley laughter faded into memory, and the hum of Juliana's car engine was the only sound between them. They went to an ice cream shop and then made their way back to Eliseo's house. They stayed in the car as they ate their ice cream. Neither made a move to get out. The moment asked them to linger.

Eliseo's spoon scraped gently against the side of the paper cup. He broke the silence first. "I had fun. Thank you."

Juliana smiled without looking at him. "Imagine how much fun I had as the winner."

He shook his head, thinking about her victory dance and gloating. He had always liked it when she won things — when her face lit up like she was the greatest thing since sliced bread.

"Hey, do you ever still play?"

Juliana blinked, turning to him. "Play what?"

"Volleyball."

"Not really. Not anymore." She shrugged. "Quince has been bugging me for lessons lately, though. Apparently, there's this boy at her school who plays, and she wants to impress him."

"She's strategic. I respect that."

Juliana rolled her eyes. "She's ridiculous."

"No," Eliseo said, his voice warm and honest. "She's just someone trying to get noticed. I get it."

Juliana looked at him curiously. "You sound like you're trying to impress someone, too."

Eliseo looked out the windshield as he remembered himself years ago. "Back in high school, there was this girl… she was pretty and loud and popular. She forgot to do her homework all the time, so I let her copy mine. She loved my mom's cooking, so I brought her extra food from home. And she hated reading, so I read to her whenever she asked."

Eliseo watched as Juliana tilted her head, her expression slowly shifting from amused to realization. "Wait, me? You liked *me*?"

He laughed short and embarrassed, and ran a hand through his hair. "Yeah. It was hard not to like a clear future Olympic winner." He thought this would amuse her further and provoke more teasing, but instead, Juliana went quiet and looked down. Eliseo hesitated. "Hey, it was a long time ago. I wasn't trying to make it weird. I knew you and Anthony—"

"No, it's not that. It's just… I probably hurt you a lot more than I realized."

He hesitated at that. "It's old history." But even as the words left his mouth, they tasted like something half-true.

"Eliseo," she said softly, something weighty in her voice. "I'm really sorry for every time I didn't see you."

That landed deep. In some hollow place he'd never had the words for. He wanted to tell her it was fine. That it didn't matter now. But it did. Something in him needed to hear that.

So instead, he exhaled, long and low. Then he reached across the console and took her hand. It wasn't meant to be romantic. Just connection.

"Thank you for seeing me now."

18 | JULIANA

The bell above the flower shop door jingled softly as another customer stepped out, leaving behind a trail of crisp air and the faint scent of cinnamon from the nearby bakery.

Juliana leaned on the counter, grinning at her phone as she texted Eliseo. It had been three days since they went bowling. Since she stumbled, and he caught her. Since the air between them shifted. They hadn't stopped messaging each other and talking since.

She didn't know what they were and what they were becoming. But she liked it. She liked the way he made her laugh, even over text. She liked how he remembered things about her from all those years ago. And she liked how she was feeling. Happy.

"Talking to Eliseo, are we?" her mother said as she passed by with a clipboard in hand and a smirk tucked into her cheek.

Juliana looked up too fast. "I know other people, you know."

"Avoiding the question. That's suspicious behavior. You're not hiding something, are you, Juliana?"

Heat crawled up Juliana's neck, warm and sudden. "I'm going to get that other order ready," she mumbled, tucking her phone in her pocket and disappearing into the back room.

Her mother had been teasing her about Eliseo lately. It was like Juliana had a big sign on her forehead that said she was talking to him. It was awkward, but that only seemed to amuse her mother more.

What was she even embarrassed about? They were just rekindling their friendship… right? The confession was about the high school version of her, not her current self. She had no reason to be blushing.

She told herself this again as she bent over a bucket of freshly delivered tulips, trimming stems and pulling off leaves that would rot in water. Her hands worked automatically – cut, strip, arrange – but her mind wandered back to her time with Eliseo.

Honestly, she hadn't planned to stay long that day. Just a short visit, a little comfort, a way to make things right between them after the fight. But the hours had stretched as they went bowling. They'd laughed about ridiculous things, like his awful aim and how she tripped over her own shoe. And then there was that moment...

She reached for the lilies next, trying to ignore the smile tugging at her lips.

Their time in the car was just as interesting. Eliseo had fallen asleep in his seat, not even ten minutes after they talked. She'd still been holding his hand when his breathing shifted, and she heard light snoring. He must've been really tired.

She hadn't moved at first. Just sat there, watching him. After a few minutes, she reached over with her free hand and moved the empty ice cream cup from his lap. Then she reached up and her fingers grazed his hair. She hadn't meant to. It was muscle memory. Back then, his hair was longer and messy, and when it covered his eyes, she would move it out of his face. His hair was shorter now, but still soft...

The tenderness of it startled her.

Her hand flew back to her lap like it burned her. Heat flushed up her neck to her face, and she sat there, pulse steady and loud.

Juliana sighed at the thought and dropped the trimmed lilies into a waiting vase. Her cheeks still felt warm at the memory. Everything was starting to feel alive again.

Colors seemed brighter lately, and music sounded different. She even opened the curtains of her bedroom to welcome in what little sunlight they had. All this because of Eliseo?

They were both older now. Changed. Single. The thought surprised her. How real it felt. How not impossible.

Juliana shook her head, trying to clear it. This wasn't the time to dive into that. She was still healing. He was, too. She wiped her hands on her apron and then grabbed the vase to take it to the front.

She felt her phone vibrate. Immediately, she put the vase down and looked, expecting another text from Eliseo. Instead, it was from her mother.

When you're done thinking about Eliseo, can you bring the order up front, please?

She groaned, heat flooding her cheeks again. "Mom…"

19 | ELISEO

Eliseo lay on his bed, his fingers loosely laced behind his head as he stared up at the ceiling. The script for the next season sat unopened on the nightstand beside him. The sleek manila envelope had arrived that morning with his name printed neatly on the front. He'd carried it to his room like it was radioactive, and it had been sitting there ever since, untouched.

He knew what was inside. Lines. Stage directions. Emotional beats and plot twists that weren't real, but still managed to bleed into the bones.

He could already feel the weight creeping back on him. The fake smile. The charming flirt. And that scared him more than he wanted to admit. Because here, in this sliver of borrowed time, he felt like himself again.

He let his head roll to the side, his eyes catching on the edge of his phone. It had been his distraction. Talking to Juliana became his favorite thing to do over the past few days.

It had started off slow. A "good morning". Then a few jokes and memes about the bowling fiasco. But now, it was every few hours. Small things. Big things. Random photos. He liked how close they were becoming.

But the countdown had started. Filming resumed in three weeks. His manager had already emailed about coordinating media coverage. His socials were buzzing again — fan accounts reposting a photo someone took of him at the coffee shop. The noise was growing louder, and he knew it would only get worse.

His phone buzzed. Eliseo sat up and grabbed it, expecting Juliana, a little flutter rising in his chest. But when he unlocked it, the message wasn't from her. It was an unknown number.

Don't freak out. It's Quince. I stole your number from Juliana's phone.

And don't worry, I won't give it out to anyone. I just wanted to say thanks.

Juliana's been smiling and laughing more. You're bringing that happiness back to her. So whatever you're doing, keep it up.

Eliseo felt a warmth build behind his ribs. He hadn't realized it showed that much — that maybe he wasn't imagining the spark that had started to flicker back to life in Juliana.

Who knows where it'll lead…

He considered Quince's messages before finally texting back.

Thanks, but we're just friends. Nothing like that.

The reply came instantly, like she was waiting for it.

It can be more. If you listen to me, I can help.

Eliseo stared at the message for a while. A part of him wanted to shut it down. Play it safe. Leave things as they were. But the other part – the part that couldn't stop thinking about Juliana – was curious.

I want you and Juliana to be happy… I also want you to endorse my hotels when it's time, so we both win from this.

What kind of help are we talking about here?

Another instant reply.

Let me plan something.

A real date. Not a 'let's just hang out and pretend we're not feeling things' kind of thing.

You don't have to do anything. I'll fix everything and I'll make sure it's secluded enough so you don't have to wear a mask.

Eliseo ran a hand over his face. This felt like a bad idea. Too soon. Too risky. Especially in the hands of a fifteen-year-old.

Almost as if she could read his thoughts, she sent another message.

I may be young, but I know Juliana better than anyone else. I'm the best avenue you've got. Trust me.

20 | JULIANA

Juliana felt like a fool as she watched Quince drive off. There she was, standing by herself in front of a little restaurant at least forty minutes away from home. Quince had told her they were going to drop off some flowers for a special wedding anniversary event at a fancy restaurant.

Juliana didn't think twice about it. She assumed her mother relayed the message to Quince because she wanted her to tag along. And she assumed Quince insisted they dress up to match the occasion in hopes that the couple would leave a big tip. But after she got out of the car, Quince yelled "You're welcome!" and hit the gas, leaving her there, confused.

It was only when Eliseo showed up, looking equally as nice, that she understood what had happened.

Her niece was going to pay dearly for this.

Juliana glanced down at herself, suddenly self-conscious. She'd worn a navy blue dress, simple but pretty, paired with her nicest boots. Was it too much? Or not enough?

And then there was Eliseo, walking toward her, looking just as nervous. Juliana felt her heart squeeze at the sight. His jacket was nice, a dark charcoal color that looked good against the light brown of his skin. His button-up shirt was a little wrinkled, and his hair was slightly messy like he'd tried to tame it with fingers and no mirror but given up halfway through. Somehow, it made him even more endearing.

"Hey," he said, smiling. "You look beautiful."

Juliana ducked her head, a shy smile playing at the corners of her mouth. "Thanks. You don't look bad yourself."

For a moment, they just stood there, awkward and warm and unsure. Eliseo laughed under his breath and moved forward, opening the door for her. "After you."

Inside, the restaurant was cozy, lit with soft amber lighting that made everything feel smaller and safer. Only a few tables were occupied, each one tucked into little nooks separated by tall plants and flickering candles. The hostess led them to a corner table.

Juliana sat with her hands clasped so tightly in her lap that it took effort to uncurl her fingers. Eliseo slid into his seat across from her, and for a while they said nothing, just looked at their menus, occasionally glancing at each other and trying not to laugh when they were caught.

It felt ridiculous. And perfect.

"So…" Juliana finally said, clearing her throat. "Did you know this was gonna happen or are you just taking this really well?"

"I knew. Kind of." He rubbed the back of his head and smiled like he was thirteen. "I wanted to hang out with you again, and Quince offered to make it happen," he explained. "She stole my number out of your phone, by the way, so you might want to change your passcode."

"What?" Juliana frowned. "Wait until I get my hands on her…"

"Go easy on her. After all, she put this together for us."

"Big deal. We could've set this up ourselves." She scoffed. "You know she tried to do this with my mom? It was a disaster."

"She set Ms. Ward up?" he asked, leaning in with curiosity.

"A food delivery driver. She swore it was fate and thought he was perfect for her. My mom couldn't figure out why he kept lingering every time he delivered food. Turns out Quince had told him she was interested…"

The conversation continued, meandering through other embarrassing stories, old memories, and dreams they didn't have names for yet. Juliana found herself leaning in, chin propped on her hand, soaking in every part of the moment.

There was no way she was falling for Eliseo. This was just a rekindled friendship and healing past wounds. So what if he was attractive? So what if he was single? So what if his little touches electrified her? That didn't mean anything. Just like when she went to his social media and scrolled through all his pictures with his co-star, Sophia, to see how close they were… it meant nothing.

It was while waiting for dessert that Eliseo's gaze shifted sideways. It lingered with concern.

Juliana noticed. "You okay?"

He blinked and then dismissed it with a smile. "It's nothing."

Then desserts came. As they ate, Juliana thought that maybe, just maybe, she could get used to moments like this. Laughing over stolen bites of cake and teasing each other with exaggerated critiques like food critics on TV.

But then she saw the same concern pulling his gaze off to the side again. Something was clearly on his mind.

She set her fork down. "Seriously, Eliseo, what's wrong?"

He looked like he was going to dismiss it again, but when he met her gaze, he closed his eyes and sighed. He spoke carefully. "The new season is starting soon."

It took a moment for the words to sink in and what they meant. Her heart dropped into her stomach. Juliana didn't know what to say. All she could think about was that he was leaving. Leaving this fragile little world they'd started rebuilding together.

"Oh," she said finally, swallowing down the disappointment.

"I don't know what to do… it's like everything is getting louder. When I'm with you–" He cut himself off, shaking his head like he was embarrassed. "I'm happy. I can think and be myself. I don't want to lose that."

The confession sat between them, raw and real.

"Then don't."

He was quiet. "It's not that easy."

Juliana's chest ached. She wanted to reach across the table. Tell him it would be okay. But instead, she leaned back, putting a small but unmistakable distance between them. Walls she didn't even realize she still had crept up out of nowhere. "Why not? You could quit. Walk away."

Eliseo shook his head, running a hand through his hair. "This is my career – how I support myself. I've got my parents to think about, and my castmates. If I leave, they'll kill off my character or worse, end the show. The director would blackball me to others. People have worked too hard for me to just… bail."

"And what about you?" Juliana asked, her voice sharper than she meant it to be. "You're thinking about everyone else. But what about yourself, Eliseo? Don't you care that this is hurting you?"

He opened his mouth, then closed it, like he didn't even know where to start.

Juliana pressed on, her heart pounding. "And–" she stopped, the words almost catching in her throat. "And what about… us? What happens to *this* when you leave?"

Her voice cracked on the last word, and she hated how much it gave her away.

Eliseo looked at her. "Juliana…" He reached across the table toward her hand, but she pulled it away.

"I'm sorry, I know I don't have a right to be upset, but I am. I thought…" She trailed off and stood up, her chair dragging softly against the floor. She couldn't look at him anymore. Not when her eyes were already burning. "We should probably go."

Eliseo looked like he wanted to say something, but he didn't know what. Instead, he reached for the bill and paid it quietly, and then they walked out to his car.

She stood by the passenger side, waiting for him to unlock the door, but it didn't happen. Instead, she felt his arms wrap around her and pull her into an embrace. She stiffened for half a breath, her body remembering to protect itself. But then she relaxed.

"Please…" He breathed out. "Don't be mad. I don't want to lose you again."

Her heart ached at that. She closed her eyes.

Why was life so complicated?

21 | ELISEO

The house was quiet. Eliseo sat on the edge of his bed, elbows on knees, thumbs absently rubbing against each other as he stared down at the floor. His phone lay beside him, the screen dark, though it had buzzed five times in the last hour. He didn't have to look to know who it was. Quince asking more questions about what happened because Juliana was upset all over again.

He didn't have an answer.

He thought of the way Juliana had looked at him after he told her about the show. Her expression had changed – gone was the girl who'd been laughing over dessert, her cheeks flushed from teasing. Something in her had gone distant.

When he hugged her, she didn't hug back. But she didn't pull away either.

She stayed.

He held onto that.

Still, the silence between them now was loud in its own right.

A knock came at the door frame, soft but firm. His dad leaned in, scanned Eliseo, and after a pause, he stepped in and sat beside him.

"I thought you were feeling better after Juliana came over the other day, but now it looks like you're hurting all over again. Talk to me."

Eliseo didn't meet his eyes. He just exhaled, deep and slow. "I'm sorry, Dad," he said finally. "It's work. And life. Everything. I've got choices to make and none of them feel right. Either way, I'm going to lose something. Maybe someone."

His father nodded once, like he'd heard this kind of ache before. In a different shape, a different time. Still, he let the quiet hold them before he spoke.

"Well, a good man asks for counsel, sure. But a wise man doesn't make decisions on his own. He gets quiet. He listens. He prays."

Eliseo looked down again.

"I don't know if I'll hear anything. I don't know if He even wants to talk to me."

"God doesn't go silent just because we feel lost. That's when He leans in closer. Or have you forgotten that He loves you and wants the best for you?"

Eliseo swallowed. "And what if I don't know how to trust Him? What if I haven't known how since Anthony died?"

A beat of silence. Not awkward. Not shameful. Just a moment breathing with transparency.

"I'm not going to pretend to have all the answers, Eliseo. I can't tell you why He allowed Anthony to die. But I can say that He's not afraid of your questions, fears and anger. You can bring it to Him, and He'll still love you and show you that He's here. You don't have to pretend with Him." He put a hand on his shoulder. "Ipagdasal mo, anak. Huwag mong kalimutan ang Diyos." *Pray about it. Don't forget God.*

After a minute, his father left. Eliseo stared at the floor for a while longer. He didn't speak. Just sat in the silence, head bowed, and heart stumbling toward honesty.

Then he whispered, "God, I don't know what I'm doing. I don't know what's right. I don't want to lose Juliana, and I don't want to keep pretending."

His hands clenched into fists.

"I'm scared. Of walking away. Of losing everything. Of not being seen. Of drowning. Please help me… tell me what to do. Show me that You're still here."

And in the stillness that followed, there was peace. Not a voice. Not a sign. Just peace.

Quiet and steady.

Like an anchor dropped in deep water.

Eliseo didn't have answers yet. But he wasn't alone in the asking.

22 | JULIANA

Juliana sat at the kitchen table, the screen of her laptop glowing against the early gray of the afternoon. Online orders blinked at her – peonies, hydrangeas, some ridiculous request for "ethereal blooms with a winter soul." She stared at the screen, fingers hovering over the keyboard, but her heart wasn't in it.

She hadn't been able to sleep last night. Or the night before. She'd gone over the date with Eliseo a hundred times in her head, dissecting every glance, every pause, every smile. It was going well. Until it wasn't. Until he told her that he'd be leaving again.

Her chest felt tight just thinking about it.

She closed the laptop, pushing it aside, and stood. Her feet moved without thought. Just trying to keep moving before the stillness caught up to her. She drifted toward her bedroom, her arms folding over her chest.

And then she saw it.

Eliseo's jacket.

Still draped over the chair near her bed. It was an aviator jacket with fur on the inside. She ran her fingers over the shoulder absentmindedly. It still smelled faintly like him.

She'd forgotten to give it back since the panic attack. She remembered the way he put it on her shoulders and spoke to her. The way he pulled her into his arms and held her. Just like he did yesterday.

At that moment, she couldn't move. Couldn't speak. Couldn't breathe.

She just let herself feel it. Her hands dropped to her sides, and she sat down on the edge of the bed, staring straight ahead. Her throat tightened. The jacket looked too at home here. Too real. Too much like a cruel glimpse of something she wasn't allowed to have.

And that's when it rose in her.

A bitterness. A grief. A fire in her chest that had nowhere to go. She stood up suddenly, as if she'd been slapped, and turned from the jacket.

Her voice came out low at first. "God… what are You doing?"

Her arms were crossed, fists clenched.

"Why bring him back? Why now?" Her voice cracked. "So he can leave again? So I can feel all of this again just to lose it?"

She laughed bitterly and paced the room like a caged thing, her words rising with every step.

"I'm trying. I'm really trying. I take care of the online shop. I go in person when needed. And I say I'm okay." She stopped in the middle of the room, staring up at the ceiling like she could see straight into heaven. "But I'm not okay."

Her voice cracked, deeper now. Like something from her chest had split open.

"Why did Anthony have to die?" she whispered, tears forming in her eyes. "Why did I live?"

The words came faster now, tripping over themselves, ragged with pain.

"You could've stopped it. You could've warned us. You could've done something. But instead, I'm here – walking around with a hole in my chest. And now Eliseo's back. And I don't know what to feel. Because everything hurts."

Her knees gave out, and she sank to the floor, head in her hands, shoulders trembling.

"I don't understand, God. You saved me… why? For what? This?"

The tears came freely now, soaking into her sleeves as she curled inward, a silent cry pressing through her whole body.

"I'm tired," she choked out. "I'm just… tired."

There was no answer. Just the steady rhythm of her breathing, slowing as the wave of pain finally crested.

And then, something quiet and deep. Like a hand on her back. Like someone was sitting beside her in the silence.

And then she heard it.

He heals the brokenhearted and binds up their wounds.

She didn't move. An unexplainable peace covered her.

Everything wasn't fine. But she knew it would be.

23 | JULIANA

Juliana hadn't stepped into a church since the funeral. She hadn't planned to that morning, either. But when her mom asked her if she'd come like she did every Sunday, something in Juliana didn't argue for once. And when she agreed, her mother didn't mask her shock well; the tears came almost instantly, though she blinked them away with a quiet smile, as if afraid one word might change Juliana's mind.

The church building was nothing like the one from her childhood. This one was modern, clean-lined, filled with glass and natural light. A large wooden cross hung center-stage, simple and unadorned. People buzzed around like bees to a warm hive, smiling and shaking hands, chatting in the foyer over coffee. There were people of all ages, all shades of skin, all kinds of stories written on the lines of their faces.

Juliana didn't know what she expected. Maybe to feel out of place. Condemned, somehow. But no one looked at her like she didn't belong. Not even the teens Quince so quickly ditched her and her mother for.

They sat near the middle. Worship was soft and steady, the lyrics full of things Juliana wasn't sure she believed but wanted to. She didn't sing, not at first, but she listened. She watched her mother close her eyes and raise her hands with serenity.

The sermon came from John 11. Juliana knew the story – Jesus raised Lazarus from the dead. It was one of those miracles they taught in Sunday school when she was young. She thought she knew where the pastor was going, but then he took a turn.

"Jesus knew He was about to raise Lazarus. He knew the ending. But when He saw Mary and the others weeping… He didn't say, 'Stop crying, I've got this.' He didn't lecture them on faith or give them a countdown to the miracle. No. He wept. The God of the universe stood beside them and cried."

Juliana froze.

The pastor's voice softened, almost breaking. "He cries with you. Even when He knows healing is coming. He doesn't rush your grief. He is in it with you."

Something deep in her clenched and then released. A sob lodged behind her ribs. All this time, she had assumed

God wanted her to get over it. To be strong. To move on. But what if He wasn't standing on the other side of her pain, shouting for her to catch up?

What if He was in it? Right there in the thick of it. Crying with them at the hospital. Crying with them at the funeral. And even beyond that situation, every moment of pain. When her father left. When Tessa left. When the depression and anxiety got worse.

Tears pricked her eyes. The sanctuary around her blurred. Her breathing hitched, and she quickly bowed her head, pressing her fingers into her palms.

She whispered, barely audible. "God... I don't know what You're doing. I don't know why it hurts so much. But if You're really here... if You're really weeping with me... then I want You in this. Please... come in. Heal me."

The prayer wasn't poetic. It wasn't polished. But it was real. And as the tears slid silently down her cheeks, she didn't feel empty anymore. She felt... held. Like someone was weeping with her. And for the first time since Anthony died, Juliana didn't feel abandoned by Heaven.

She felt seen.

24 | ELISEO

Eliseo woke before the sun did. As usual.

He drifted in and out of half-dreams, always ending with Juliana's voice echoing in the dark corners of his mind.

What about… us?

He sat up slowly, rubbing a hand over his face, his heart heavy in his chest. His phone buzzed on the nightstand. Again. It had been buzzing off and on with messages from his manager and the studio – reminders that his real life was coming back for him, whether he wanted it or not.

He slipped on a sweatshirt and walked to the kitchen, the stillness of the house thick around him. His parents were still asleep.

Eliseo grabbed a mug, poured coffee, and sat at the table. The silence wasn't peaceful. It was loud. Loud with uncertainty and fear. With Juliana's silence since their date. With the question that had started clawing at him the moment the script landed in his inbox.

His phone buzzed again. He glanced down, expecting to see his manager's name, but instead it was Sophia.

He answered. "Hey, Sophia."

"Hey," she said, her voice uncharacteristically soft and strange. "I'm sorry for calling so early. I just… I had to talk to you."

"You okay?"

"No." She hesitated. "I just had a dream about you, and I can't stop thinking about it."

Eliseo raised an eyebrow. "Okay. I'm flattered but…"

"No, I'm serious. A weird dream." A pause, like she was still choosing her words. "I saw you filming a scene, but every time you spoke, the whole set started to fall apart. The walls, the roof, the lights, everything around was crumbling, but you kept speaking… until it all crushed you."

He didn't know what to say. He didn't know what was more shocking – what she was saying or that she sounded truly disturbed.

"Eliseo, I told you before that I've seen this place eat people alive. Good people. You know I've been in this industry since I was a kid," Sophia continued, voice shaky. "I think you shouldn't do the next season. I know that sounds crazy, but that dream felt real. I woke up with this heavy and sad feeling that I couldn't shake. Listen, I care about the show, but I care about you more. I think you need to get out before it swallows you whole."

That had been the first sign.

That afternoon, he wandered outside, his mind still spinning from the conversation. He thought maybe a walk would help him think. The air was crisper now, the clouds thinning overhead. He took the long route around the neighborhood. When he passed the mailbox, he noticed a large envelope sticking out with his name on it.

It wasn't from the studio.

He opened it, confused, and found a script inside. A new one. He flipped through the pages. It was a heartfelt, small-town Hallmark-style film about a woman reconnecting with her ex. It was completely different from *Bleed for the Badge*. Tucked inside was a handwritten note from a director he'd met months ago at a fundraiser. She said she saw something gentle in his eyes and if he was ready to try something different, he should consider this.

Eliseo sat down on the curb, script in his lap.

That was the second sign.

Still, he needed more. He wanted to be sure. Too much rested on this.

That evening, he stopped by the gas station. Eliseo kept his mask and hat on as he went inside. He got in line behind a man in worn jeans and a flannel.

The man leaned on the counter, laughing with the cashier in an easy, unhurried way. "Ten years, man. Ten years, and I finally walked out today."

"No way," the kid behind the register said. "You serious?"

"Serious," the man replied, still grinning. "Woke up this morning and said, 'I can't keep doing this.' I didn't even pack my lunch. Just walked in and said I was done."

Eliseo didn't know why he was listening.

"It's scary," the man continued, shrugging as he slid a twenty across the counter. "But I knew I had to do it. I was turning into someone I didn't even like. My kid asked me the other day why I never smile anymore."

He shook his head, then laughed again. "Sometimes, you gotta walk away before you don't recognize yourself anymore."

The words slammed into Eliseo's chest before he could brace himself. They were so casual, but they clung to him.

The man turned to leave, coffee in hand, the bell over the door chiming gently as he disappeared. Eliseo watched the door swing shut. He didn't say anything when he reached the counter. Just paid. Quiet. Heavy. The cashier gave him a curious glance, but Eliseo didn't meet his eyes.

He stepped back into the night and let the cold air slap him. The sky overhead was endless and still. He stood outside the car for a moment, breath fogging in the air.

And maybe it wasn't much – just a stranger in a flannel shirt saying something to a bored teenager in the middle of the evening.

But it sounded a lot like his third sign.

25 | ELISEO

Eliseo stood on Juliana's porch, hands stuffed in the pockets of his coat.

He wasn't entirely sure how he got here. One minute, he was pacing in the driveway of his parents' house, rehearsing what to say for the hundredth time. Next, he was in his car, driving toward her house. And now he was staring at her front door, heart pounding like he'd just sprinted half a mile.

He hadn't reached out in days. Hadn't explained the silence. Hadn't explained anything. But after what God had shown him… he couldn't keep it to himself anymore.

He knocked once before he could change his mind.

The door cracked open, and Quince peeked out, raising a suspicious eyebrow. She looked him over, then narrowed her eyes slightly.

"Hey," Eliseo said, trying not to look as nervous as he felt. "Is Juliana home?"

Quince studied him for a second, then, surprisingly, nodded. "Wait here."

She disappeared inside.

Eliseo exhaled, scrubbing a hand through his hair. His heart was slamming against his ribs now, and all his carefully composed speech dissolved the moment he heard soft footsteps returning.

The door opened again, and there she was.

Juliana.

Her hair was pulled back into a puff. She wore a sweatshirt and leggings, looking half-curious, half-cautious. Her eyes landed on him, and for a moment, neither of them said anything.

And then the dam broke.

"I prayed," he blurted out. "A lot. And I don't know how to say it, but God gave me these signs. Not subtle ones. Clear. Like billboard-in-the-middle-of-the-highway clear. And one of them was this ridiculous movie offer – total rom-com, I'd be wearing sweaters and rescuing dogs, nothing like Anthony. And Sophia, out of nowhere, tells me she had a dream and that I should quit. Just like that. And then at the gas station, this guy starts talking about how he quit his job and felt freer than ever."

Juliana opened her mouth, but Eliseo kept going, helpless under the flood.

"And I prayed about you, too. About us. Because I didn't want to leave without giving you an answer, and I'm sorry for–"

"Eliseo, slow down. What are you talking about?" She stepped outside, closing the door gently behind her. The porch light cast a soft glow around them. "What happened?"

Eliseo stared at her for a long moment. His chest rose and fell. "Na-miss kita."

Juliana stared at him. "What does that mean?"

"I missed you."

Juliana's eyes widened slightly. She nodded, small and vulnerable. "I missed you, too."

Eliseo's hands twitched at his sides, wanting to reach for her, but he didn't. He wasn't sure he was allowed to yet.

"I quit the show," he said again, slower this time. "I'm done. I think it's the right thing. And I feel like I can breathe again."

Juliana's mouth parted slightly. "You actually quit?"

He nodded. "When I prayed, God gave me so many signs that this was what I was supposed to do."

They started walking slowly, moving down the street, their feet finding rhythm on the pavement. He told her about the conversation with his manager and that he had to go in person to handle the contract stuff. He also told her about the new role.

Eliseo spoke again, quieter. "I prayed about what to do with you, too. And I felt like God told me to be honest. So… here it is. Spending time with you made me realize that I still have feelings for you. Even after all this time. Something about you just has a hold on me. I'm really sorry about how dinner ended the other day. If you can forgive me, I'd like to try dating."

Juliana was quiet for a few steps, processing. Then she asked gently, "But what about your new role? Don't you have to go back to L.A.?"

"Yeah," Eliseo admitted. "But the new project is slower. More flexible. I'd be back and forth, and we could visit each other. I know long distance isn't ideal but…"

"A long-distance relationship might actually be good for us," she said, cutting gently across his sentence. "It lets us keep growing. With God. With each other." She added, "I've been reading my Bible again. I even went to church with my mom and Quince. It felt like God met me in the middle of everything. I think I'm in a good place now. Not perfect, but healing."

Something about the way she said it filled him with hope. "That's good. Really good."

They'd made their way back to her house now. She stopped at the bottom of the steps. Eliseo was amazed at how easy everything flowed. They didn't dance around the fact that they had feelings for each other. The idea of long distance didn't put her off. Everything was working out.

Eliseo felt a confidence come over him. "So… does that mean we're officially dating?"

Juliana looked down, shyly. "I guess so."

He stepped closer, testing the waters. "Yeah?"

She looked up, and before she could answer again, he kissed her. It was gentle at first. Just a question pressed against her lips. And then she kissed him back. An answer against his. And for a moment, they engaged in a beautiful dialogue.

From the window above, they could hear Quince squeal. "Finally!"

Eliseo and Juliana broke apart, laughing as their foreheads bumped.

He scratched the back of his neck, sheepishly. "I should… probably go."

Juliana smiled. "Probably."

He lingered. So did she.

"I'll text you," he said.

"Okay."

They stood there another beat, not quite ready to go, but knowing it was time. He turned, slowly heading down the walkway. When he glanced back, Juliana was still on the porch, watching him with that same quiet smile.

Eliseo felt the peace again.

26 | JULIANA

"Well, someone woke up on the right side of the bed. Humming and everything."

Juliana hadn't even realized she was humming until her mother said so. She quickly dropped the tune, half-shrugging as she poured herself a glass of juice. The last thing she needed was to give her mother another reason to tease her about Eliseo. "Just a good day, that's all."

"A good day," she repeated, giving her a knowing look.

Just then, Quince swept into the room like a tornado in fuzzy slippers and dramatic timing. "Good morning, everyone!" Her gaze landed on Juliana. "I bet it's especially a good morning for you."

Juliana shot her a look, but said nothing. She hoped that would be enough to deter her niece, but she should've known it would have the opposite effect.

"Juliana and Eliseo sittin' in a tree," Quince started singing, "K-I-S-S-I-N-G…"

Juliana shot her another look. Sharper this time. "Quince. No."

"First comes love, then comes marriage…"

"I'm warning you."

"Then comes an interview on daytime TV." Quince cackled, sliding into the chair across from her.

"You are done for."

"I regret nothing. I worked hard to get you two together. I deserve this."

Juliana saw her mother turn to her slowly. "Wait, what's going on? Are you and Eliseo dating? Officially?"

Juliana looked away, sheepishly. "I was going to tell you. Just… later."

Her mother's expression softened, and her eyes glossed over. "Oh, Juliana." She crossed the kitchen in two strides and wrapped Juliana in a tight hug, arms warm and strong. "I'm so happy for you. And so proud of you."

Juliana blinked hard, the emotion catching her off guard.

Quince also seemed surprised. "I hope I get this response after I start dating Mark."

"You've come so far in just these two weeks," her mother continued. "I see it in your eyes. There's life again. Hope. God is doing something in you, honey. I prayed for this, and He's answering. He always does. Never stop praying." She sniffled. "I half expect Tessa to come through that door."

Juliana swallowed the lump rising in her throat. She opened her mouth, not even realizing what she was about to say. "Mom… I was going to do something really stupid, and I'm sorry. Thank you for praying for me."

Her mom kissed the top of her head. After, almost giddily, she went back to the stove. "I think we need to have Eliseo and his parents over for dinner soon."

Juliana noticed Quince slowly backing away from the table. When they met each other's gaze, she bolted.

Juliana was after her in seconds, chasing her down the hall and through the living room before finally tackling her onto the couch in a tangle of giggles and elbows.

"Pinned," Juliana declared.

"I'll scream," Quince muttered, breathless. "The neighbors will call 911."

"I don't care. You went through my phone, you tricked me, and now you're teasing me." Juliana stared down at her niece, who was squeezing her eyes shut in preparation for an attack. As Juliana watched her, something tender filled her. She ruffled Quince's hair gently.

"Thank you."

Quince opened her eyes slowly. "For what?"

"For being your chaotic, loud, ridiculous self. You helped. More than you know." Juliana hesitated for a second. "I'm really glad you're here. Not just as my niece, but as my little sister."

Quince's eyes widened just slightly. She blinked like she didn't know what to do with the compliment, but Juliana could tell it hit deep. Eventually, Quince smirked, shrugging off the softness. "Well, duh. I am awesome."

Juliana laughed and finally let her up.

After that, they went off to get ready for their day. Juliana was half dressed when her phone buzzed on the nightstand. Her heart did a little skip as she glanced at it. Eliseo.

Good morning. Sleep okay?

She smiled, typing back.

Good morning. Yeah. You?

Woke up thinking about you. Haven't stopped, actually.

Corny.

I prefer the term romantic. Wanna come over? My mom made a pretty big breakfast. We can eat and read the Bible together.

She stood there for a moment, thumb hovering. Before she could type anything, another text came through.

Yes, I'll read.

She breathed out a laugh. She finished dressing, grabbed her keys, and headed to his house.

His mother opened the door for her and smiled like she already knew. She didn't say much, just pointed toward the table and started fixing a plate.

She and Eliseo ate slowly, the way people do when something good's happening and neither of them want to break it. After, they drifted into the living room, tea in their hands and Scripture on their laps.

Juliana listened to Eliseo read. When he finished, she was quiet for a moment. "I like doing this with you."

He looked at her. "Me too." A pause. "You know, it was so hard to pray after Anthony died. I couldn't even read the Bible. And it's still a little hard to talk to Him, to be honest," Eliseo continued slowly. "But being around you and my family makes it easier. It's hard to explain, but when you're around, I'm reminded God exists. I feel like I can heal properly."

Juliana's hand reached out, gentle and unassuming, resting lightly on his. It wasn't dramatic. Just steady. His thumb brushed gently against her knuckles.

He looked like he might lean in, just slightly, but before the moment could unfurl fully, footsteps approached.

His mother appeared in the doorway. "I never thought I'd see the day," she said, smiling like a sunrise. "My son and a beautiful woman reading the Word together in my living room."

Eliseo groaned, sinking back into the couch. "Ma…"

She waved him off, undeterred. "I'm just saying," she teased, "after years of praying, I might actually get my grandchild."

"Ma!"

Juliana sputtered into laughter, trying and failing to hide it behind her hand. It seemed her mother wasn't the only one who was enjoying this.

And just like that, the day began.

With scripture.

With laughter.

With love blooming quietly between them.

27 | JULIANA

Everyone stood near the boarding gate, surrounding Eliseo. The flight to L.A. was already blinking on time behind him in bright blue letters, but no one seemed in a rush to say the words that would send him off.

His parents moved first. His dad pulled him into a strong hug, and his mom cupped his cheek. They shared some words in Tagalog with each other.

Eventually, Eliseo backed up. "I'll call you when I get there."

Juliana's mother stepped forward next, her eyes carrying the shimmer of emotion she didn't try to hide. "Thank you, Eliseo," she said, pulling him close. "You really are a lighthouse."

He smiled, earnest. "Thank you, Ms. Ward."

Then there was Quince. She hugged him hard and then pulled back with a grin. "Just remember to throw my name out every now and then, so people will remember it when I build my hotels. You owe me."

"Of course."

"Good." She gave his arm a playful jab.

Then it was just Eliseo and Juliana. The crowd drifted around them, all rushing feet and voices and the clatter of wheels. But for them, they didn't hear any of it.

Juliana looked at him, memorizing his face and the way his presence made everything in her feel a little more anchored. Somehow, in three short weeks, he'd slipped back into her life like he'd never left, and now she wasn't sure how to let him go again.

She reached up and brushed her fingers through his hair. "It's gonna be weird not having you around."

He caught her hand and pressed it to his chest for a moment. "I'll be back. I promise. And in the meantime, we'll call, text, and do video calls. Maybe I'll write you letters."

She tilted her head, a soft smirk playing on her lips. "Letters?"

"I'm romantic like that."

She laughed gently. "I think you mean corny like that."

"I'll come back soon," he said again. Not as a maybe. As a promise.

She believed him. But it still hurt. She thought long distance would be good for them, but she didn't realize how hard it would be, and he hadn't even left yet.

"I'll be here."

Eliseo bent down and kissed her, soft and sure, like a promise sealed in warmth. When he pulled back, her eyes fluttered open, and her smile trembled but didn't break.

Behind them, Quince made a dramatic squeal, and the others turned quickly, pretending not to have been watching. Pretending not to be grinning.

The final boarding call came over the speaker. Eliseo reached for his bag. Juliana's hand lingered in his one last second, and then let go.

He pulled his mask up and stepped away slowly, looking back and waving after a few feet. He paused before turning the corner, locking eyes with Juliana one last time.

As Eliseo disappeared from view, Juliana let the quiet fall around her. But it didn't feel empty. She could still feel his warmth in her hand. His words in her heart.

Her mother touched her shoulder gently. "You okay?"

Juliana nodded. "I am."

Because this goodbye didn't feel like an end. It felt like a beginning.

EPILOGUE | JULIANA

Six Months Later

The airport was loud. Announcements rattling overhead, kids crying somewhere near the baggage claim, and the steady rumbling of rolling suitcases. Juliana shifted her weight from one foot to the other as she waited excitedly by the arrival gate.

It had been three weeks and four days since she last saw him in person. Not that she was counting.

Normally, Eliseo visited twice a month. A few days, sometimes more if filming wrapped up early. But this month had been different. Delays, reshoots, and long nights on set had stretched his schedule thin.

And now, finally, he was coming back to her. At least for the weekend.

She had another reason to be giddy. A secret she'd been holding onto for weeks. It had nearly slipped out more than once on the phone, especially late at night when his voice was tired and soft and the distance between them felt bigger than it was. But she'd held it. Saved it for this.

The second she spotted him walking out, her stomach did a little flip. He was wearing a hat and mask as usual, but he was slightly broader than before. His frame had thickened. His arms were bigger. But the gentle look in his eyes hadn't changed.

And when their eyes met, his smile came easily.

Juliana walked, then jogged, straight into his arms. They didn't say anything for a moment. Just enjoyed the embrace.

"I missed you," she murmured into his shoulder.

"I missed you too."

Eventually, she pulled back and looked him over. "Wow. You weren't kidding when you said you needed to beef up for this role."

He smirked. "What are you talking about? This is exactly how I looked the last time you saw me."

She rolled her eyes, smirking too. "What mirror were you looking in?"

Ten minutes later, they were in her car, windows cracked, and radio low. Juliana drove them to the restaurant he took her to when he'd first come back. It didn't look much different than before. But this time they were different.

Eliseo ordered a burger and fries, and she went with a grilled cheese and sweet tea.

Conversation came easily. He talked about his latest project, how the protein shakes made him gag, and that the costume designer kept calling him "Emilio".

She told him about joining the volleyball league at the nearby rec center, Quince changing her mind about the name of her hotels, and Tessa calling and promising to visit soon.

They were halfway through the meal when Juliana stopped eating and looked down at her sweet tea. Her fingers traced the rim of the glass.

"Eliseo," she said slowly.

He glanced up.

"There's something I've been waiting to tell you in person," she tried to keep her tone casual.

His eyes searched hers. "Okay..."

"You remember when I told you my mom's been wanting to open a second flower shop location? And she wanted me to run it?"

"Yeah."

"Well, at first I didn't know if that's what I wanted to do, but I thought about it and prayed, and I finally told her yes."

"That's great." He wiped his hands with a napkin and then reached across the table and laced their fingers. "I'm proud of you."

"Thanks." She nodded. "I started looking earlier this month, and I found a place."

"Where at?"

She bit her lip. Her eyes shimmered with a mixture of nerves and joy. "It's in L.A.," she said, finally. "I sign the lease next week."

For a full second, he just stared. Then he sat back, a grin breaking across his face. "No way! You're serious?"

"I'm serious."

"You're moving to me?" he asked again, like he needed to hear it twice just to believe it.

"I feel like this is the right thing for me. A change of scenery, running the business, and we'll be closer to each other."

He started rambling, clearly happy and unable to contain it. "This is awesome! I'll show you to my favorite spots to eat, I'll introduce you to my co-stars – Selena too, she's been wanting to meet you. I thought this wouldn't happen until we got married …"

She watched him ramble on with a smile. This side of him – excited, scattered, rambling – was one of her favorites. Not the polished actor the world saw. Not Justin Lee. Not Anthony. Just Eliseo. Sincere. A little awkward. All heart.

Suddenly, he stood up, came around the booth, and slid in beside her. Then he leaned over and kissed her. And she melted into it like she did every time.

Six months ago, she was sitting on the side of a bridge, her pain louder than her hope.

Now?

She was healing. She was learning. She was loving again and allowing herself to be loved.

She was letting God peel back the layers of hurt and plant new things. Everything wasn't perfect. Some days were better than others. But there was an unwavering light in her. Laughter in her voice. Purpose in her days. And faith.

Not all manifestos are made of ink. Some are made of grace, second chances, and love.

Eliseo and Juliana's story is fictional, but healing is real. If you're walking through a dark season, I want you to know that healing is possible through Jesus. He's closer than you think. He healed me from depression, anxiety, loneliness, low self-esteem, and more. I am a living testimony that Jesus heals. I invite you to pray with me below if you'd like to experience healing as well.

Prayer:

Jesus, I don't want to carry this pain anymore. You said, "Come to Me, all who are weary and burdened, and I will give you rest." (Matthew 11:28) So I come to You now with all of it – my wounds, my past, and my fears.

You see it all. You've always seen it. And You still love me. "You have seen my affliction; You have known the distress of my soul." (Psalm 31:7)

I renounce every lie I've believed. That I'm too far gone, that I'll never heal, and that I'm alone in this. In Your name, Jesus, I break every chain the enemy has placed on my life. "For the weapons of our warfare are not of the flesh but have divine power to destroy strongholds." (2 Corinthians 10:4)

Holy Spirit, come into the places that hurt the most. "The Lord is near to the brokenhearted and saves the crushed in spirit." (Psalm 34:18) Fill every crack with Your peace. Cover me with Your presence. Remind me that I am Yours.

Thank You for dying for me. Thank You for rising again to give me life.

I believe You can heal me, and I trust You will. "He heals the brokenhearted and binds up their wounds." (Psalm 147:3) In Your name, Jesus, I pray. Amen.